AGE OF PERIL

Greg and Kathy Weller

AGE OF PERIL

a fantasy by
Greg and Kathy Weller
(authors of Poetically Together)

Sometimes the big adventures come to
the biggest heart in the weakest frame

Published by: ADVANTAGE BOOKS™ www.advbookstore.com

Library of Congress Catalog Number: 2022946047

Names:	Weller, Greg, Author
	Weller, Kathy, Author
Title:	*Age of Peril*
	Greg & Kathy Weller
	Advantage Books, 2022
Identifiers:	ISBN (print): 9781597557061, (mobi, epub): 9781597557160, (hardcover): 9781597557306
Subjects:	Christian Life: Inspirational

First Printing September 2022

22 23 24 25 26 27   10 9 8 7 6 5 4 3 2 1

Table of Contents

SECTION 1: DOCTOR & SON

1: RISE AND SHINE 13
2: CLOUD UP 13
3: EGGS 15
4: DEAD CAT 17
5: NEXT WAKENING 17
6: SCHOOL MA'AM MOONLIGHT..18
7: GIGGLES 20
8: CHASE-EE...21
9: HOW MANY PINPOINTS OF LIGHT DANCE ON A LAPEL PIN?.....................25
10: MORE 28
11: THE CONE OF FRIENDSHIP...29
12: MIRRORS AND FAKES 30
13: TO MARKET, TO MARKET..34
14: BEES..35
15: DEALS 36
16: THE STAND...37
17: NEW TIMES..40
18: DOCTOR DAGGER...40
19: DARKNESS 43
20: VIGIL 45
21: SOLACE 46
22: ADDITIONAL 46

SECTION 2: AIDER AND ADDER

23: INTROIT...51
24: REVISITED...51
25: HOMES AND THUNDER..54
26: `STORY: THE FIRST..55
27: TALES..56
28: STORY: THE SECOND..60
29: AMAH'S PRICKLES...61
30: STORY: THE THIRD..62
31: AMAH'S FIRST DAY 64
32: STORY: THE FOURTH 67
33: STORY: THE FIFTH 68
34: TAHLA EXPOUNDS...69
35: ON ANOTHER WORLD, ANOTHER BELIEVER 69
36: A GOOSE BY ANY OTHER NAME STILL. 72
37: STORY: THE SIXTH 75
38: STORY: THE SEVENTH...76
39: STICK GROPES THE MEASURE...78

40: TAHLA EXPOUNDS II 80
41: A BETTER GOODBYE 80
42: BIRD AS HAWK 83
43: TAHLA EXPOUNDS III 85
44: SNAPPETS 86
45: STORY: THE EIGHTH 87
46: THOUGHT 88
47: TAHLA EXPOUNDS IV 88
48: TAHLA EXPOUNDS V 89
49: THE CALL 89
50: SITUATION OF INTEREST 90
51: STORY: THE NINTH 93
52: TAHLA EXPOUNDS VI 94
53: STEPPING UP 95
54: BALLS THAT BOUNCE 96
55: WRITING HOME 98
56: TAHLA EXPOUNDS VII 98
57: KEEP YOUR GUARD 99

SECTION 3: FIRE NIGHT

58: LURKING DEAN 103
59: "WE LISTEN, WE HEAR" 103
60: TAHLA EXPOUNDS VIII 104
61: THOUGHT 104
62: TAHLA EXPOUNDS IX 104
63: TAHLA EXPOUNDS X 105
64: BREAKFAST SONG 105
65: SNAPPET II 106
66: THOUGHT 106
67: PREPARATION 106
68: ONWARD LIKE JELLY 106
69: WHISKERS ARE CLOSE 107
70: JELLY 109
71: JOURNAL OF P ULYSSES PLUGRATH III–ENTRY 125 110
72: JOURNAL OF P ULYSSES PLUGRATH III–ENTRY 125 POSTSCRIPT 111
73: MOPPING UP 111
74: THOUGHT 112
75: TAHLA EXPOUNDS XI 112
76: JOURNAL OF P ULYSSES PLUGRATH III–ENTRY 126 113
77: WAVES ROLL 114
78: THOUGHT 114
79: NEW ACQUAINTANCE 115
80: RESPITE 116
81: JOURNAL OF P ULYSSES PLUGRATH III–ENTRY 127 117
82: EVERYMAN'S CALL 117

83: INTERLUDE...118
84: JORT SPEAKS 119
85: THOUGHT 119
86: NEWS COMES UNEXPECTED 120
87: JENNY'S PLAYTHING...121
88: WITH THE CHOIR...122
89: THE JOURNEY 125
90: JOURNAL OF P ULYSSES PLUGRATH III–ENTRY 128.............125
91: AFTERMATH 125
92: ANOTHER MATH..126
93: MINUS THE ONE 126
94: JOURNAL OF P ULYSSES PLUGRATH III–ENTRY 129.............127
95: MRS FALPUB REMEMBERS.......................................127
96: JOURNAL OF P ULYSSES PLUGRATH III–ENTRY 130.............128
97: ALLA-WUZ REMEMBERS THE BULLY........................129
98: QUICK NOW 130
99: JORT STEPS UP..132
100: UN-SEEKING ALLIES...132
101: JOURNAL OF P ULYSSES PLUGRATH III–ENTRY 138 134
102: SUGAR TEARS 134
103: UN-SEEKING I 134
104: UN-SEEKING II 134
105: UN-SEEKING III 135
106: ALLA-WUZ MISSES 135
107: TUMBLE FROM DEPRESSION 136
108: TUMBLE, AS PARENTS, FROM DEPRESSION...........136
109: THE WANDERERS' BATTLE.....................................139
110: TUMBLING–IN 141
111: JORT SPEAKS II 141
112: PEELING BACK TO SINGLENESS 142
113: THE BETTER UNDERWEAR 143
114: JORT SPEAKS III 143
115: ALLA-WUZ TUMBLES INTO DEPRESSION, MEETS "THE POWDER" 144
116: AMAH, UNDER THE ARC, STANDS ABOVE THE ARC 145
117: FORCE 147
118: LEACHED LITANY 148
119: GREY AND WHITE...148
120: HOUSE CALL...149
121: JORT SPEAKS IV 150
122: ALLA-WUZ MEETS AN OLD FRIEND........................151
123: MEETING...152
124: WORLDS IN A CLICK 154
125: LOSTNESS (MRS FALPUB SPEAKS)........................157
126: JOURNAL OF P ULYSSES PLUGRATH III–ENTRY 140 157

127: TINCTURES... 158

128: PRECIOUS *(A FRIEND OF AMAH'S FAMILY SUFFERS)* 159

129: SCHEDULED TEAM... 160

130: OPEN HOUSE... 160

131: THE BETTER WIDGET 161

132: VALOUR 162

133: DAY OUT 165

134: JOURNAL OF P ULYSSES PLUGRATH III–ENTRY 142..................... 166

135: HERITAGE 166

136: CHORES... 168

137: ORTHINOR 169

138: STORIES AT THE INN... 170

139: SLEEPY 176

140: BREAKFAST... 176

141: A PREVIOUS EPOCH 177

142: NEXT DAY 177

143: SNAKE PLAN 178

144: FIREBOMB 179

145: MIDDAY NIGHTDREAM 179

146: GROUP... 180

147: SWARM 180

148: THE STAND... 183

149: AS UNKNOWN AS CATS 185

150: WIT'S END... 188

151: 'NEATH THE SWARM.. 190

152: A FAREWELL 192

153: GREY ON GREY 193

154: MOTHER SPIT 194

155: JELLY SET... 195

156: AT THE LAST 197

APPENDIX 199

COMMENTS AND KEYS TO "TAHLA EXPOUNDS".. 199

SECTION 1

DOCTOR & SON

Please note: this book is written in a very unusual style. It's really helpful to read the chapter titles. They may be your only clue as to who the chapter is about or to the location of the chapters actions.

Greg and Kathy Weller

Chapter 1
RISE AND SHINE

Morning kisses my head like a mother.

Blinking, I stumble to my feet, and stagger to the table

The sunlight crouches in anticipation at the door along with my friend. Seeing me, he smiles and shows me proudly his crop of potatoes.

It's hard growing potatoes behind your ears. Go to sleep and you wake, and there's breakfast–have them boiled, roasted, as fish and chips!

The day seems to pulse adventure and the unturned stone, the neighbour's locked shed, and the dark furled cloak of a stranger striding confidently, yet cautiously, down my street. So I gulp breakfast, half listening to Mum and Dad growling about something to do with rent.

Up and at 'em, I say. The world needs needers and I scuttle out the side door to a bigger sky.

CHAPTER 2
CLOUD UP

Alla-wuz and I bounded down the street.

We'd known each other for years. Our families were friends too.

It was a morning that hugs you hard, that makes you fall in love with summer. The firebirds climbed into the sky and swooped the way they do each summer–speeding downwards at great speed, the wet dye in their wing feathers boils off into the air, leaving a shimmering curtain of reds or blues behind them. As we watched, above the park a red male and blue female firebird spiralled downward in a trailing vision–spirals and fractals hung and glimmered in the air. Even the Benfords stopped to look, and they hold nothing beautiful but new things, Ma says.

Surpassing the hot bitumen streets, we reached the park. Stepping past the egg-like mound of dirt on the footpath, we suddenly sprinted down the short footpath and into the park proper. Alla-wuz trumpeted softly in pure excitement. Above, the pair of firebirds dived, and curtains rippled and shimmered in the air. Arching their backs, they swooped towards a copse of trees and sped down, down, down towards the soft yellow of the flowers under the trees. Down, down, down, and a sudden turn of their wings just at the last second and miraculously they sped away, somehow still in one piece.

There was a loud rough laugh from the shadows under the spreading branches of the copse. Then out came a group of three. They strode confidently and, if someone's style of walking could be described as having such an attitude, sarcastically, across the open area of the park. They seemed to be heading towards an area for public speaking. Their shadows as they walked seemed to have a life of their own, sometimes running before them, sometimes cavorting off to one side, almost trying to leap off the ground like a small dog leaping into the air—all this, while the sun hung still in an azure sky.

There was another egg-like mound close by, and one of them bowed in a mocking way to it, snickered loudly, and then they reached the Speaker's Stand.

Smoothly they went into action, a well oiled machine. Their shadows behaved themselves as the owners opened suitcases, erected fold-up tables, donned capes and pulled out a couple of mirrors which flashed brightness at me as it caught the rays of the sun. The sun hung, seeming to lose energy. Somehow all the vibrance seemed now to come from their corner.

Curiosity hit me like a surfwave, then drew me like the undertow between your toes as the water sucks back into the reaches of the deep—a desire to know about these people turned my feet that way. I had taken only three steps when I felt Alla-wuz's trunk wrap around my arm. "No, Amah," he said. "Let's play upstream."

The words took a long time to reach my ears and hit them without excitement, like being hit with wet paper. But . . . he was my friend, so I sighed, and turned with him on a darkening morning.

In the middle of the park was the Upstream. The water flowed down from a drifting cloud—a creek full of sparkling, splashing water pouring down in playful vigour from the edge of the cloud towards the waiting ground, which drank it in thirstily. But there was a way upwards too. On one side the water frothed and gurgled and spiralled up. We giggled, plunged in—and up to the top. We crawled onto the cloud, and lay there in the sun. It had found its strength again, and we lazed there on a perfect summer morn.

Presently, we stirred, stood up, and looked around. Cloudland was beautiful as ever, stretching the full and usual hundred metres. A tree strode towards us and as it bowed, it offered us its fruit. We each took a perfect pear, and the tree strode onwards, exulting in the morning.

Alla-wuz jumped, just for fun, over a sleeping sunbeetle sprawling on its back. It was only the breadth of my hand wide—quite a small one. As Alla-wuz jumped over it, ears flapping as if he were trying to fly, a fresh potato fell from behind one ear and thudded very near the sunbeetle. It opened its eye in the midst of its belly, saw a tonne weight in the air above it, and its wings sprang out so hard as to push it off its back and into the air, and it fled (it must have thought) for its very life.

I knew where I was going, too. I moved compulsively to the edge of the cloud and wriggled myself forward slowly, belly hugging the soft firmness of the cloud until my eyes peeked over the edge.

I looked down at Speaker's Stand.

Chapter 3
EGGS

Smoke poured from the front of the stage and glided around the first rows of the audience. My eyes opened wide. Jack Benford was there in his newest, newest clothes–his nicely combed hair under the cute hat his Mum had bought him. I had wanted that one last Saturday, and there had been a few tears on the shop floor before I had left with a shattered dream. Here he was, my age, with gifts rained down on him by a family who "sneezed money wherever they went", Ma says. He seemed entranced by what was happening on stage. And when I looked, I could see why . . .

Tricks glissandoed off the magician's fingers–the appearing flower, the disappearing rabbit, the lady being cut in half, and then the wound disappearing.

The crowd seemed to be as puppets. The magician walked forward they leaned back. He was suddenly soft and coy–they leant forward eagerly. There was a murmur, then a laugh at a strange disappearance of a coin–then suddenly each person felt a coin in their pocket. They pulled it out and waved it excitedly each one to his neighbour, and the shadows of the three slipped off the edge of the stage and seemed to play festively around the hands of each joyous one.

My next-door neighbour rushed across the park from the road. He hastily found the ticket-keeper, the stick-man of the three, paid no money but took a small tablet offered him, gulped it down, and rushed to join the crowd.

The ground bent softly beside me as Alla-wuz also edged closer to the edge. We both watched.

"Dad told me, Amah," he said breathlessly, "that the tablets are magic. Every now and then there's a bad one. It makes you wet like a two-year-old in bed. It gets worser and worser, and then all the water's out of you, and you die."

I rolled over and stared at him. His father was important–he locked people up for bad things. He should know about such things . . .

"He says at the end there's nothing left but a dried-out thing like a potato chip." I turned back to gaze at the three of them below. Two were there on the stage, and the shadows seemed to be in a tiny huddle in one corner of the stand. Then I saw the other, off to one side. He had a red firebird in his hand, and he suddenly snapped its wing. The bird screeched as he dropped it.

As he walked back to the stand, wiping red dye from his hand, the firebird was walking in smaller and tireder circles.

"He says that some try to stop it. They make a hole in the ground, put in a blanket which keeps the water in, and they can lie there and soak in the water that's come out. Put another blanket on top, and cover it with dirt put on it by friends."

I was about to scoff when there was a thunderclap from the Stand, and the show had finished. People spilled every whichway on their way home. They chattered quietly, some were subdued.

There was a loud yell from one, looking alarmed and clutching his pants. A dribble had formed there, and found tiny spaces in his clutching hand. Down it trickled midst a swell of laughter from those nearest. Startled, he glanced around–then glanced up and somehow straight into my eyes.

My next door neighbour. It was my next door neighbour.

Then he bolted, heading across the park, across the street, and down onto our street. There was wet on the road.

I blinked, and looked around at Alla-wuz. "Why do they do it? Why do they come– it's so dangerous . . ."

Chapter 4
DEAD CAT

There was a man who saw a billboard advertising a juggling act. "Doug–a cut above the rest" the notice read. It took his fancy, and so he went.

Arriving late, he searched in vain for a good seat, but all that was left was the front row. In his enthusiasm he gladly moved down to the front and sat right in front of the juggler. The juggler juggled with balls, he juggled with skittles, he juggled with hammers.

Then he brought out three chainsaws and turned them on. Calling for absolute quiet, he started to juggle. The audience was rapt. So too the man in the first row, leaning closer and closer to the stage.

The artiste started to breathe deeper and quicker, a slight sweat starting to form on his furrowed brow. Then the furrows turned a mile deep, and he sneezed the way you sneeze after the first spring cleaning . . . And the chainsaw threw up in the air, and spiralled down towards their target. The first row!

The first one cut a shoelace, the second arrived .025 seconds later and carved the hood off his jacket.

The third bounced off the other two, and gave him a short-back-and-sides.

Moral : Curiosity comes a cropper more than once.

Chapter 5
NEXT WAKENING

I woke suddenly. The sun itself had finally had thoughts of rest, falling towards the horizon. The cloud lay as firm as ever under my back.

Alla-wuz breathed slowly, a little distance away.

I found footing and shook him urgently. We were very late and I thought with dread of Mother's tears.

We dashed to cloud edge, slid downstream. Back on normal ground, we walked briskly, each towards his respective thunder and warmth. I saw occasional splashes of wetness as I walked.

Finally I reached my place and stepped carefully over the wet area just between the footpath and my property. The stray drops continued on, traced an urgent pathway themselves–leading clearly and inviolably to the neighbour's front door.

That night, as I lay awake, I thought I could hear, from the neighbour's backyard, the rasp of shovel and the grunts of someone nearly exhausted.

Chapter 6
SCHOOL MA'AM MOONLIGHT

Nights and nights later, I sat at my window watching. I imagined police chases coming down the main road and swerving into our street: the villain with glazed eyes and panting lungs–but always caught. Then the road became a river, and the slave traders came, gathering up the Pepper People like they did ages and ages ago. Dad had told me that, in his dad's time, the Pepper People were captured and kept because they grew peppers in their armpits. (When they raised their arms, you could always smell it on a hot summer's day–it was said by the slavers that the smell proved they weren't people: just things, cattle, slaves.) Why, Tahla across the road was one, but now he was free, even though people looked at him strangely sometimes. Alla-wuz's people, with their potatoes went free, but Tahla's people hurt, suffered, were killed, for the sake of the peppers and the backs of their females– backs covered with soft fluffy tails, which the ladies of other races used to make into hats.

I could see Tahla come down the stairs and into his kitchen–his house was just across from mine. Both were nice two-storey comfy houses.

Tahla found a cup in the kitchen cupboard, flicked away a nuisance pepper, and drank deeply. I suddenly wondered if he could see me at my second-storey window, but realised my bedroom light was off. Safe!

We both stared out our windows into the moonlight, in no hurry to go anywhere. Bed was an eternity of prickly heat and elusive sleep that hovered on the corners of the eyelids, never quite pulling them down.

I stared at the moonlight pouring down onto the street. Moonlight was a grumpy woman, who drained away the bright colours and made everything the washed-out colour of grandmothers' clothes, pales and pastels and pallidness. Even the trees had lost their joy and stood stiffly in the breezeless night, standing a little taller, a little sterner, like little kids before a irritated school-ma'am. No relaxing under her rules, just a interminable waiting . . .

It was still. The dogs in the distance barked mutedly, a little over-awed by the grumpy pale woman. So quiet, I thought that even the listening devices that dad had put in our garden to let us hear, to protect us, wouldn't hear anything. If I were to go downstairs now and get the headphones . . . I could bring them up here and just listen! But even they would be stunned into silence by the moonlit schoolma'am. A bird on a tree in the street started to move a little, then thought better of it.

I had just started imagining a new slave drama—the police discovering the traders raiding a party of pepper people when there was an actual movement on the street, and one of the strange three stood at the corner of our street. Moonlight was at his elbow, splashing blacks and deep blues into the pale ribbon that was my road.

Slowly he sticked down the street—like a collection of sticks which were scarcely on speaking terms with each other, his arms and legs moved in the same direction roughly at, but not exactly at, the same time, like a marionette operated by an amateur. He proceeded down our street. Moonlight continued to drain colour from her surroundings.

He was mystery, a world of the new and wild, a book of yawning promise that could take my soul and tumble it. I could almost feel the dark and a lightning flash, a call in the midst of a fragile hope, and I wanted to learn.

But Tahla was quicker. He slipped out his front door, and scuttled, scampered, glided to Stick's side, and they paused outside my house. Talking of who knows how and when, pauses of promise and interest, of pathos and comic anticlimax. I needed to hear!

I needed the headphones!

I opened my door quietly, twisting the knob finger-width by finger-width, round and round. Then through! . . . and along the padded hall floor, past Mum and Dad's room—I heard them giggle to each other in the dark—and there were the stairs. The stern carvings on the banister poles looked at me, and I felt the heat-fear on my skin, then it was gone. When I was young, I had been so scared of those twisted carved figures on each pole—I had known they were destined to stalk me always. . . But that was three; at four years of maturity I knew they were wooden.

And so, down the stairs, past the cellar entrance with its strongroom and locks from the Trouble Days, and into the kitchen.

Headphones . . . headphones.

Then I had them, a quick fiddle to see they were working.

Into my ear, Tahla said, "It's so fun hahahahahahaha."

Perfect. I could hear crystally clearly. The six listening places outside were working. And up the stairs, into the room, and to the window.

Chapter 7
GIGGLES

"It's so perfect. A new toy. A mellifluous melody of mayhem. . . ."

Tahla, I could see, nodded rapidly. "Like my brother when he comes home to visit. It's so exciting. I like the moonlight, even."

Moonlight stood sternly.

"Watch, my young . . . friend. Wait till someone comes," and they hunkered down in the shadows under the shrubs and trellises in my garden.

I had dozed a little, when a voice bellowed in my ear. "He's coming, young . . . friend," and I jerked upward to find that the stick thing had spoken, and the headphones were working fine–

Down the street came a walker. He walked gingerly under the moonlight, when a bubble, green and glowing, wobbled out from whence the two hid. It reached the walker's arms, brushed against it, popped, and green splattered his jacket sleeve.

The green seemed to wriggle, and suddenly it was gone. The walker jumped jerkily, then clawed at his coat. Off it came, and there was a frantic scrabbling at his sleeve button.

Up it was pushed, and there, having soaked through all those layers of clothes, was the green. The skin glowed green, and bubbled a little.

The walker screamed, and ran, leaving his coat behind.

Giggles and snorts came through my headphones.

Silence again. Then in the far distance, I could hear a car. The sound teased the senses, then grew louder, always louder, approaching, approaching.

It turned our street, and came down it.

Stick-thing shot, and green flashed in thorough the open car window, smearing a face. I saw a hand grab at a green skin which was seeming to tighten.

The car wobbled through a few yards, then seemed to speed up. Down, down the street, around the corner, a scream, a crash, a cry.

Giggles.

Moonlight strode purposely street-long, around the corner, and then returned, looking sternly satisfied..

Chapter 8
CHASE-EE

"Fun can be had more fully fledged by coating completely someone. Let's wait. A walker comes soon, surely."

And the clock coaxed itself slowly round the dial while the two figures waited, waited, wasted an hour.

"My young . . . friend, try now. Run, and I'll chase you. Pause, and face the green goo. Run, and be free, be safe. Try it now."

There seemed to be a push, and Tahla stumbled out from the bush, stood near the stern moonlight.

There was a sudden bark from the bushes, full of a fury and anger such as ever a father could never muster. "Run," and it carried all the horror and terror of a thousand crying soldiers.

Tahla burst into motion, ran half the street at a sprint. I heard a voice from way away, from a house near him, "Get home, you fool. It's dangerous out," and Tahla mock-bowed, and bounded up the hill, as if heading for home.

Then a sudden detour, and he was buried deep within my garden. Puffs, pants and a chuckle came from the headphone.

Stick yelled, "Bang! Could have gotcha," and Tahla bounded away into the darkness of the neighbour's yard. Yet somehow Stick was there before him.

A mad bustle, a joyous swerving, and exulting in the movement of body and bone under the clear will of its owner, and Tahla was on the statue in their garden, posing as an extra figure. In the moonlight it was exquisite, so flawlessly joined.

Stick cavorted down the street, took aim, shot from behind the boy.

Suddenly his leg glowed greener than Spring's arrival.

Tahla giggled, ran. Back into my yard, and the stars seemed to pulse happiness and a promise of excitement.

He hid at the corner of our house, roughly under my parent's windows—their snores drifted out on the air.

There was a soft pop. Then he staggered out, his leg glowing.

Moonlight looked impatient, and sternly raised a finger.

Tahla ran glowing into the middle of the road, panting. There seemed to surround him and me a cold voice, "Run, little stripling," and there was a deadness in the sound. Green hit him in the chest, disappeared quickly 'neath the clothes.

Tahla jerked into a frantic sprawl and clamber. Legs pounded and he was under his own house, and I could see him frantically sweeping dirt up and over the glow.

He lay: watching for green, scooping up dirt.

He reached out surreptitiously to scratch the leg. A long scratch, and I could almost feel all the hunger you ever felt, all the thirst you ever endured, all the desire of love from your parents, all was in that scratch. The moving of fingernails hard against the skin, and fulfilment.

A quick covering with dirt.

Another frantic scratch, and covering.

A scratch at the back, then at the leg. Cover and pause.

He jerked upward, scratching frantically everywhere.

Three green pulses from behind thudded into him, and he was off and running down the street. Green everywhere, bubbling and soaking. Seeking the skin, finding, it. Then the itching, and a tightening, like a bearhug, everywhere on the back.

His foot hit a stone, and he was sprawling on his back, eyes looking up at Moonlight, standing stern, merciless.

Green pulses. Up and down the front. Quickly, like sprinkling with salt.

Stick stood above him, grinning. Moonlight stood like a kindergarten monitor.

"Hey . . . friend."

Tahla grinned.

"I'm so mis . . . understood," and Stick stretched out a hand to the green, semi-human thing on the ground.

It reached out its hand and was pulled upright. It stood, a little shakily.

Stick put an arm around him. "I'm so, so misunderstood," and he smiled.

He shot a green bubble into the air.

It drifted in the air, and in its sparkle and reflected charming glow was all the beauty of the words of its owner, all the excitement of Speaker's Corner, all the vigour, the hope, the thrill of tonight's chase. . . .

Promises radiated from it, like glory from a sunset.

It floated down gently on a subtle breeze. Down, down above his head. It filled with rainbows, held all the fragrance of a bag of lollies.

It touched the top of his head.

Balanced. Didn't burst.

Stick smiled.

Moonlight walked forward imperiously.

Tahla smiled, looked up at the beauty above him.

The edge of the bubble rolled down his forehead, tumbled down in slow motion over his nose, and paused.

It balanced gently on the tip of Tahla's nose. Stick stepped forward and blew gently on it.

Moonlight started a perverted pirate's jig.

The bubble changed slightly and began to sink—over the nose, over the cheeks.

Tahla pretended to waddle like a seal holding a ball on its nose.

He slapped his hands together, like a seal and its flippers. Behind him, Moonlight began to cartwheel.

Tahla waddled, and the bubble wriggled, slipped down further to hug his ears.

It was like looking through a magnifying glass. Stick looked so big, and his smile grew and grew until it seemed to fill the sky.

The bubble gently reached the back of his head, then slipped a little further.

His whole head was inside, and he seemed to be mouthing, "I'm a goldfish."

Stick blew on the bubble. Moonlight leapt, spun.

The glistening canopy shrunk to cover the skin below it. As Moonlight pirouetted, the green chemical reached the skin and hugged it with warmth, warmer than the warmest summer, firmer than an adult's handshake, squeezing, squeezing. The green on the arms, legs and torso felt like fire now, hugging tighter than last year's clothes, pressing the skin, firmer, firmer.

Bearhugs now, bearhugs, hurting, and Moonlight ran gently, pushed off as an acrobat, gracefully into the air.

Trembling now, a trembling in all the bones, the skin squashing in a frantic striving to escape the pressure from above.

Escape, escape.

A popping of the bones. A reverse somersault nearby, acrobatic, elegant.

For Tahla, a feeling like a vehicle moving, rolling, crushing the covered green, and red and water ran swiftly down the gutter, away, away.

Moonlight cartwheeled with agility down the street. She let out two whoops like a slaver with a catch.

The green contracted. Water ran.

The green was not a person now.

Moonlight danced, and the green compacted until the size of a small dog.

Contracted, until the shape of a black box full of secrets.

Contracted—until an acorn-thing.

And it stopped.

Stick bowed to it, mock-ceremoniously, reached back his foot, and kicked it. It bounced and rolled down the street. Stick reached it, and kicked again.

The sound of kick and tumble echoed slowly, farther and farther into the distance.

Behind him, the gutter stopped gurgling.

Moonlight paused, slumped a little, and began to follow. Then turned in Wagner's darkest fashion and gathering the folds of her sternness around her, a last glance at the street . . . Her eye passed over my window, then paused, locked on my eyes. She strode purposely down the street, over the fence, through the garden, and I could hear the trellis rattle under my window.

Hide, escape, escape. And I rushed to my bed, curled into a ball under the blanket and froze, all movement fleeing my limbs. The thought pounded, "Is the window shut? Is the window shut?" but no movement from hands, from fingers, from eyes. The cellar with its locks and concrete was the only safe place, but I could not move. The moment paused, hungry for blood. It paused for hours.

After an eternity, it started to rain, washing away the terror and moonlight with big drops.

Chapter 9
HOW MANY PINPOINTS OF LIGHT DANCE ON A LAPEL PIN?

A new morning ran over my eyelids, awakening me. The night before stung my eyes as I got up. A quick look at the locked window, and downstairs.

The sun lay luxuriant on the steps, and soon Alla-wuz and I were on the way to the park. The norse were there—great muscled animals. Onto their back! and I walked on norseback around the fences for a blessed eternity of mobility, height and harnessed strength.

Alla-wuz, too heavy for the norse, cheerfully made his way to the painting area, found an empty spot. He luxuriously filled his trunk with paint, and shot it at a waiting canvas. A sign above the area proclaimed, "Make a picture, take a picture, hang it in your home."

Alla-wuz put the canvas to one side, grabbed another, and prepared himself.

His mother always groaned about having more pictures than space on the wall. But one look at the soft elephant eyes and the drops of yellow, red and green at the tip of the trunk, and "I always melt", she says forever to my mother. (When I had first heard it, I checked carefully after she left, but I could never find any water left from under her feet when she walked.)

At Speaker's Corner, separated from me by a whole park and an eternity of fun, the three were preparing. Meanwhile, my norse snorted, grabbed another handful of food with its feeder hands, and eyed off another one approaching too close the food trough. Under my legs, muscles tightened like trap springs. A harder breath from the norse started a nervous reaction in my stomach, when from one of the streets near the norses came a strange sight.

A man, or so . . . He was of usual height, well dressed, had a suit (with a flower and a lapel pin), shiny black shoes, neat hair. But under the suit, his shoulders seemed to ripple and rub muscle against muscle, a giant whose shoulders might hold the world. Alert eyes atop a nose like an eagle, a man of sight, a man of action as needs.

The other norse wandered away, and the norse muscles straining against my legs relaxed slightly. I blinked in relief, and in the blinking it seemed that the image of this man, this doctor (I guessed, because of his bag) hovered yet in my closed eyes. He was surrounded by pinpoints of light, swarming, dancing, circling him, it seemed, in awe.

He walked closer and closer my fence, and I could see a crack in the ground near me tense itself, if such a thing could be, close itself up, and pause. On he came, and I was close enough to see the satchel—a doctor's bag indeed, from its contents. And on and on he walked–surrounded by the pinpoints, tiny gold pulses in a bright day–each pulse had the joy and the beauty of ten thousand summer days distilled into a tiny dancing spark.

On and on, and looking down near his feet, it seemed that the grass near his feet looked like millions of one-armed creatures trying to clap, each with its neighbour's hand. And striding and striding . . . then past.

The grass near me stilled its applause, the crack re-appeared. I looked up to see I was now looking at a large back. The sparks danced closer and closer to the doctor as he walked now through small groups of people, on, on towards Speaker's Corner. A small stream broke the ground nearby–a newly-born rivulet chased the downward path laid by by-gone actions, raced down the grooves, racing towards the nearby street.

I could see Speaker's Corner starting to throb with the excitement of the regular afternoon show.

The Doctor reached one of five mounds scattered across the park. He lifted the shell on a pool of glistening water, and on a tiny withered moving thing, moist. I instinctively held my breath, fearing the blast and onslaught of the stench which must be rolling from the pool.

But the Doctor leant down, said something, and a glistening thin arm came up, strong as marshmallow, robust as a wafer, up and up into a muscled hand. A brief meaningful look between their eyes, and the being sprang up, withered but with thickness growing on the bones, muscles budding, blossoming, tautening, as I watched.

He sprang up, then paused in mid-hop, paused, a capsule in time, paused suspended in a bubble of time that never moved. "It's sufficient for the disease," the Doctor seemed to say, and moved on.

He strode on, the scene repeated at each of four more mounds: lifting the mound, asking permission, the raising up, then the suspension of time–I guess, until a better fix.

Then he reached the crowd gathered around Speaker's Corner. And I suddenly away from Norse Corner, up upstream and to the corner of the cloud nearest Speaker's Corner.

I could see from my vantage point that the Doctor looked briefly at the three on the stage–and somehow they paused, one in mid-action of magic flags appearing (appearing, it was now obvious, from up a sleeve), one in mid-contemptuous smile even as a shadow moving away from him was in mid-leap into the audience. The shadow hung, suspended like a falling bat. The third of the three, Slime, had paused too in mid-theatrical flourish.

Time wore on and they did not move.

The audience was not affected, however, and the Doctor turned to them.

"Once upon a time, there was a wood carver, famed in all the land as a master craftsman of toys. One day, he crafted for himself a three-inch little wooden boy, and being a master craftsman, of course, the boy came to life. He was still wooden, of course, with the strange

affliction that, if he did not daily apply the woodcarver's oil, his body and limbs would suddenly grow disproportionately so that one leg could be desperately long, or an ear ridiculously swollen whilst a finger could be just a toothpick.

"He desperately longed to have the woodcarver's skin—but instead he was a toy, just a three-inch toy—just like all the other three-inch toys the woodcarver was so fond of making.

"He managed to keep his thoughts and longing to himself, though, and pretended obedience to his master. Soon, the master, so proud of his great creation, put the wooden boy in charge of the other toys, in charge of all the many toy soldiers, in charge of the toy music bands, and even in charge of the master's own jewels, to keep them safe from any rat or covetous hand which might come near. But his desire was always on the woodcarver's skin— to be human, to be the equal of the woodcarver.

"He struggled to gain influence over the other boys, and soon he gathered a small group— not nearly enough, but a start. Soon, there may be enough to quell the woodcarver. As he struggled, it was of course necessary to show his rebellion to the other toys, so he willfully avoided the oil. And so one foot swelled and swelled while the other leg lengthened and lengthened. Soon he was unable to stand in public queues, or to play football.

"His hands and face grew, and it became painful to walk in crowds, to nod his head if there was someone in front of him. And as things got longer, they got thinner and thinner— so he had quite the thinnest nose and thinnest right big toe. Soon there were more and more painful squeals as he walked onto buses, visited shops, bought groceries.

"The other toys he had persuaded also grew thin and lopsided, so slowly the rebellious toys gathered together, being too entangled when in anyone else's presence. Noisily, they moved from the woodcarver's studio, to the long cupboards under the kitchen sink. They could be together, avoiding the squeaks of pain, being with like-minded people.

"And so . . . they came to hate the woodcarver, and made plans for his destruction. They carved masks, each one gaily showing a different form of death, and their eyes looked out midst a sea of blood, or a blackness of a strangulation scene painted on the masks. But useless plans were everywhere; no plan was ever perfected.

"And finally, in frustration, they found that skewering the woodcarver's ants in the ant farm was the only thing they could do. And they did it, with malice abounding.

"Beware the three, like children with pins and needles, they sting, pain, and would kill those lesser . . . But always, always they are afraid of fire.

"And you must choose between them and the woodcarver."

Away the Doctor, walked, passing through the crowd, out of the park, heading downtown. Behind him the newly created stream ran its way through the pond and gurgled down gutters, cleaning them, carrying little pieces of rubbish into the drains.

As he passed onto the street, I thought I could once again see the pinpoints swirling round him. A dog ran from a yard, charging him, barking…

One of the pinpoints nearest the dog scooped near the ground, grew, became in an instant a muscled giant, proud, and with such a pure light that the sun blushed, jealous. It moved toward the dog, which yelped, and ran like frantic tumbling thought into its own yard.

The figure shrunk, became a pinpoint, and continued its dance of light.

Chapter 10
MORE

There was a boy who thought, "There must be more". He resolved that rules need not stop him, and so up one night and out the window. The night lay innocent and naive before him. And he pounded through neighbor's backyards, stole three oranges from a tree just outside the back door, gulped them down, and left the peel on the ground as a clear sign of invasion. He spun a street sign around so the main road seemed to point into his neighbour's yard; he put a firecracker into the other neighbour's letterbox so it exploded showering metal into the air, and then fled whooping into the night as the lights turned on. He climbed into another yard, searched for rocks in the rockery and pulled back his arm to hurl thunder at their roof, when a vice-like grip entwined itself into the muscles and nerves of his leg. He looked down at a large dog, and somewhat in shock he dropped the rock, and the dog, hit by accident by the rock, yelped and disappeared into the distance. He staggered to the fence, somehow over it, and into safety. But falling badly, he sprained an ankle. Fire danced along his nerves with every move. He lay there hour after hour, colder and colder, unable to move—he even had to let go in his pants.

At the first callings of the dawn animals, shame drove him somehow to make the trip home. Somehow under the fence, somehow along the street, somehow to the front door of his house. Just as he got there, the door opened and his father dashed out, having just noticed the empty bed.

He carried him inside, cleaned him of every spot of dirt, bathed him and placed him in a bed of healing.

Moral: God is the ultimate Good Samaritan.

Chapter 11
THE CONE OF FRIENDSHIP

Once upon a time there was a pine tree which loved the people around it. It loved them so much that every year when a certain season came around, it would produce presents–they would lie under the tree in tinsel, in beautifully wrapped ribbons and festive paper. And children would come and carry away things of joy, things of hope, things of love.

But there was another tree in the forest, and its heart was mean, more hurtful than a spider, and grumpier than the dog down the street. It wanted people to come near it, but when they reached out to touch it, it would quickly wrap its branches around the outreached hand and squeeze hard. Quills would push hard into the hand with a pain like the very worst prickle. The tree would let go, and children would go away crying.

Soon people learnt to avoid the tree, and would gather instead around the giving tree. When they opened their boxes from under the tree, there was even more love than before, the presents were more wonderful, the batteries lasted longer and the parts in them never broke.

The mean tree grew angry that no one came to visit it. Everyone knew how much it hurt. So it slowly crept near the other tree. Nearer and nearer, until it could put its branches into the other tree. It quickly and happily turned its branches to be alongside the other branches, looking just the same. So when children and adults came to the good tree and found such beautiful things as would make your heart ache for sheer happiness, they would reach out to touch the tree and would often find the mean tree's branches. Quickly, the tree would squeeze them hard, and they would walk away, howling from hurt, from pain, and from being so surprised that from the good tree could come pain, sorrow and hurt.

Soon many people didn't come at all to visit the good tree because they were puzzled, their feelings were confused, and wasn't there always something else to do on Present Day anyhow?

The good tree grieved to see how much the mean tree had hurt, had deceived . . . had succeeded. So he thought of a new plan.

Next season, when the people looked at the area where the good tree grew, they found near it a forest of small saplings. The good tree had cloned itself. Around it for as far as the eye could see where row upon row, column and column of copies of the good tree.

Each had a bow around it, and a note saying, "I am the good tree. Take me home. Let me grow in your house always."

Chapter 12
MIRRORS AND FAKES

I crept to the edge of the cloud, crawled and wriggled on my belly the last few handbreadths until I could see over the edge. I was sickened to see the three setting up their magic show.

Around them a crowd was gathering. Mothers were smoothing blankets on the ground, fathers and children were to-ing and fro-ing to the toilets, friends were greeting, and expectancy hung in the air, building like an inflating balloon.

But there was a second crowd sitting apart, looking away to the south-east, looking towards the direction from which the Doctor had come. They waited while the heat of midday passed and was blown away by the cooler afternoon.

Behind them the magic show had been set up, and places were taken. Nauseated, I craned my head towards the Doctor's hoped-for entrance point, and I saw the park had changed.

It had become a thriving fairground. Sideshows marched in regimented fashion between hot-dog stands and fairy floss providers. All stood in silence–stretching in silence to every corner of the grounds.

On the stage, there was a drum roll. The magician cleared his throat dramatically under the bright stage lights which stared down at him.

"Ladies and gentlemen, all the fun of the fair." He gestured grandly at the carnival, and held the pose... Then the stage lights went dark. The three walked off the stage and into Sideshow Alley.

Suddenly, as if a switch was thrown on, music came from every entertainment, flashing lights powered over the teenagers' scary fast rides, popcorn popped, butter sizzled, and a thousand packets of fairy floss were opened.

The crowds gaped, then slowly drifted to see, to examine this great spectacle.

And every ball thrown in the alley was lucky, every air-rifle found its mark, every clown's head held the balls in their throats until they could all spew out at once into the highest score. Game conspired against game to give away a bigger and bigger prize, a better sample bag, a larger dagwood dog. Merriment rose on the air. Smiles abounded.

Suddenly someone called out, "the Doctor! The Doctor!" and many craned their heads to look. The Doctor turned the corner wearing a cloak over his head, and they cheered, when from the other side of the fair came a faint call, "The Doctor! He's here. Welcome back, Doctor." And from a third direction, a fourth way, a fifth path came the calls, like confused birds calling to each other in a fog that obscures all vision. And now the calls came from everywhere, a hundred voices battling against each other to be believed... and a hundred doctors wandered up and down Sideshow Alley like tourists.

As the town clock struck 2:30, its sound coming to us on the breeze, the Doctors went into action.

A Doctor flexed his muscles and talked of a will to fight, of armed resistance. Another ran up onto the stage, conjured with his hand, made a tiger disappear, and it came back a lion... Another Doctor, his assistant, brought a fox out onto stage. He conjured and they multiplied, one after another coming from behind the swirls of a magician's cape. More and more, and they ran off the stage, a snarling yammering pack.

Doctors passed through the audience, passing out tablets.

Three Doctors entered stage right as the other Doctor walked away, taking the fox. The new ones went into a yip, yip, yip routine slapping the back of each other until they fell over, dodging a pole swung by one of them, almost being poked in the eye but for a hand between the approaching fingers.

In the middle of their act, a Doctor ran onto the stage, and glanced with fear behind him as the pursuer climbed onto the stage–it was a Doctor! Frantically, the Doctor catapulted off the front of the stage onto a tightly clumped section of the crowd–who caught him (just)–except one who yelped, then hopped around on one foot. The chaser teetered on the edge of the stage, scared by the jump. A call came from behind the stage– no, under it–and a trapdoor opened in the floor, and a Doctor with a moustache scrambled up from below, yelling angrily at the teetering figure, who overbalanced and fell off the edge of the stage. The man scrabbling out of the trapdoor caught his foot on the edge, and his nose collided with the stage floor. Undaunted, he up, rushed to the edge of the stage, jumped vigorously off and belly-flopped onto the Doctor lying on the ground, where they tumbled and shouted at each other. The magician, the Stick and Slime returned to the stage and commenced a startling cavalcade of illusions–the metal rings, the lady walking though the wall, the finding of the audience's card and fifty dollars to boot (all returned to the audience), and a appearing pill in every pocket of every amazed member of the audience, the levitating glass of water, which suddenly appeared near those who seemed interested in the tablet and it tipped begging them to drink, the pounding of a drum as each impossibility performed on the stage built on the previous one–until no one was surprised to see the three performers' shadows leapfrog across the stage, then hover and move in the air to make a halo play around each head...

Just as the show was building to its loud festive ending, three people and one Doctor twitched, tumbled to the ground and made sounds of ecstasy and singing. Each one had eaten one of the new tablets. Five more fell from the same complaint–the number seemed to build moment on moment, quarter hour on quarter hour: a paroxysm shook each minute two more. They seemed caught up in an ultimate delight, like the feeling of six summer songs rolled into one, a tasting of fruits none had yet imagined.

A different Doctor moved through the crowd and touched each one, as blades of grass near his feet clapped hands, each one with its neighbor. If the sufferer looked into his eyes, the person seemed to pause, then to move extremely slowly, so that a wave of a hand in rapture would take a year, a standing and falling an eternity.

I smiled. I could see the real Doctor was here! He was continuing to work.

And over to one side I noticed a boy towering high, young like me–I'll be five soon–but so tall. Looked just like the Doctor! He watched his father with a proud smile on his face, eyes satisfied. Then the lad moved, too, out into the midst of the activity, grass dancing at his feet. He too began to move through, slow timing those in extremis, telling them to look forward to some future time.

The Doctor and his son were at work!!

There was a false Doctor nearby, cartwheeling along while a few people continued to watch him and smile. He did a handstand, raised one hand off the ground and waved nonchalantly to the passing children whilst he slowly bent the other arm–down, down, down, and up again he went. Almost as amazing was a medical imposter three metres away (on the other side) of the true one. He somehow reached behind passing children's ears and brought out a large balloon animal–he produced dogs, rabbits, a begging squirrel as he passed through the crowd. Another invited the passers-by to throw knives at him–they hit him, but unphased he proudly protested that quality was an illusion and so his suffering was pretend. Each of the false Doctors passing through seeming to subtly come closer and closer to the true surgeon who was busily aiding those in need.

Suddenly one Doctor threw two knives in the air, one to each of the other pretenders, and they rushed, knife high, at the true surgeon. When they reached him, one step away, arms almost in a downstroke, a frenzy of slash and sever, about to shade all with red, the whistling downward of a shiny death, when the knives were almost there, the Doctor disappeared. All that was left was a stethoscope falling to the ground in a graceful spiral.

The knives slashed downward repeatedly, unconvinced. The animal balloon Doctor pushed an animal, dark, resembling strongly the Doctor's suit, sprawled it on the ground where the real Doctor had lain, and knives raised and descended. Then the animal balloon Doctor straightened up and did a clown dance of pretend shock, hands held up to his mouth. A second Doctor held it up. It looked just like sliced clothes, sliced so finely.

He marched and paraded it all the long way up, up, up on to the stage, and stood with smiles. "See, the troublemaker has died. He tried to save others. But if you can't save yourself, what use?"

The teenage boy saw his father disappear, smiled quietly, and continued to slowtime those in need.

Yonder, two that had earlier refused his help and had let the ecstasy run its course, now yelled in pain, arching their back, lashing wildly at the sky, clawing frantically at the grass, their fingernails snapping under the pressure, leaving blood behind–then they collapsed in a pale sick bundle of confused flesh. A bystander reached in cautiously into the pile of strangeness, felt for a pulse, shouted, "I... he's... dead."

The scene was repeated, and I decided slowtiming them was the only way to help...

As the day ended, the sun sinking to rest, exhausted by what it had seen, men came and took the dead away, as the fire-dancer doctors came out.

Chapter 13
TO MARKET, TO MARKET

Hurt abounded.

A feeling like a growing cactus swelled along the length of my backbone. My face was full of prickly heat.

I was lost. All around me aisles and aisles of cans, column upon column of tall legs that looked like Mum's and Dad's but weren't. The towers on those columns seemed impossibly long, impossibly strong, and as threatening as kindergarten on that first day.

I was almost five, I thought sternly, and yet the back of my tongue seemed to swell backward, expand into the throat and hover there, an impossible boulder impossible to ignore. I tried to swallow and got somehow some fluid past the boulder. It seemed to run though to my eyes, and I sat down in a corner next to the drink bottles and howled.

I heard a soft voice asking after my health, and I looked up. Through rippling vision of blinked tears, I saw a long shape which went up and up, became a tower, became shoulders and arms, became a head. A familiar head. The Doctor!

"Don't cry. I've felt it too," came from a figure beside him—his son. Somehow it became important to be respected by these two people that seemed to care for others so much.

"I'm OK. I was just wondering what to do."

The Doctor looked a little stern. "It's alright to know you were scared. Now take my hand."

It seemed such a large hand, a strong hand, a hand that slipped my world into its own, and I knew he was a hero.

My eyes seemed to clear, my backbone a little weak from its experience, knees a little wobbly. But I was up!

And so we found my parents, and I parted from the Doctor, but I know he was fine, strong, right, and incredibly wise.

Chapter 14
BEES

Once upon a time, there was a small boy, who liked nothing better when it was hot in the middle of summer, than to go outside to where the clover baked happily in the sun. Swathe upon swathe of flowers reached up towards the warmth, and bees laboured, humming their songs of work and accomplishment and joy.

He would rush to the clover, and with his favourite shoe, would slam it down joyously, quickly, on the nearest bee.

One! Two! Three lay dead.

Soon, some of his energy gone, he searched for another. A little more slowly, he came to the next bee and slammed down quickly–missed.

Not concerned, he slammed his foot down again at the bee, which flew abruptly to one side–safe again. But adrenalin started to surge into the thrumming wings, as the black and white shoe hovered and thumped again.

The bee flew up towards the head of the one attacking him, and buzzed noisily, looking for a place to settle, to protest, to deter.

Flailing arms kept the bee away as again and again he buzzed, continually seeking and being denied.

The little boy turned and ran for the house.

Up the three stairs, like someone four years older, and in, and the screen door slammed shut.

The bee buzzed noisily, kept from its prey.

The little boy found his friend inside. Same age, but stronger, wiser.

"The bee. It's chasing me," he panted. Eyes were wide.

The other stood up and, "Don't be worried…"

"I'm not going outside ever again. It's after me."

"No, you're safe. Come and see. . ." said the other, an arm around his shoulders, and they walked down the hall, opened the screen door, and into a day full with sunshine.

The waiting bee saw its chance, dived at the movement. Landing, he plunged his sting into the other boy's hand.

The other's hand was given the sting, given the pain, given the punishment.

And the bee, having hurt uselessly, had no more sting, and went away, powerless.

Moral: A friend in deed is friend indeed.

Chapter 15
DEALS

They had him in an alley–the son of the Other was at the end of the "No Thoroughfare" lane. The three approached and surrounded him. Although surrounded by a magician, the stick figure and the oily one, the son didn't seem afraid.

They let him be in the corner, staring him down a while. Stick sprang to one side, caught a large male rat as it scurried between buildings, and sitting happily, commenced to dissect it.

The still was broken by a voice calm as the wind gently rippling wheat. "It'd be easier if you leave town now," stated the son.

Stick laughed a little too hard, so that he collapsed untidily in a corner, and had to gather limbs and jaw, had to co-ordinate them again. He stood up; his voice came out, a vicious growl, capped somehow by a frantic whine. "You slugfest…"

The magician stopped him. "Let's work together, us and yours. At the Stand tomorrow, we'll throw up fire around the stage–it'll be necessary to kill some, let's say two people–so that people there'll know it's real. Then you walk through, die, and your father, the Doctor, will rush through, heal you. And it's right, it's balanced: they'll know we are a team, us and yours."

"My parent is my parent. I'll not torment him."

Slime cleared his throat urgently, smoothly rolled over the ground, producing from thin air a collection of cakes, cakes with cream, chocolates, strawberries to make a farmer weep. Gently two identical large cakes were laid there. Exquisite candies hugged the sides of the cakes. Custard, so thick as to make gravity its very own–crept slowly down the cakes' sides, paused in exhaustion at the thick candies blocking its path.

"Look," oozed Slime, "We can talk about this. Have some cake." And he picked up with both hands one of the cakes–large enough for both a birthday and three picnics– and slid it through his shirt, through his shirt, through the wall of his stomach.

After twenty seconds his face lit up, smile upon smile–as the sugar rush swept his face. "You are Other. Don't you miss this… this rush?"

But the Son's reply: "I'm within this body, I'm within its rules–the Doctor's rules."

The magician tried again. "Let's pour understanding out on the night, coating it with right. Let us find, enter into, coalesce into a secret arrangement. Leaders of the world do this. Companies of the world pour their soul into such understandings. We too! If you see me as Lord, seek me as Lord, hold me as Lord, then I'll fall back so gently, so softly as the years fade and roll, so that you storm my throne easily, carry my body (or such a counterfeit body as to persuade all doubters) away, and rule. We as friends, you as the king. We each have our joy, neither has had the pain."

"Only my father, only him, only his ways," and the son turned and walked out. A set to the jaw and adrenalin pulsing in his walk carried him quickly past the three, past a mound. He simply touched the mound and an old grey woman arose, vibrant in the health of his giving. Another woman passing the entrance of the laneway on crutches within thirty seconds went scurrying home with good news. The son started to hum "If You Need A Revolution." He touched an acorn–it grew, unravelled, swelled, became a person dropping peppers.

He turned the corner and was gone, leaving three who glared after him. "We're gonna have trouble with that one."

"Create a couple of Universes, and you think you're almighty..."

"Hush, we'll not talk of that–not in this book."

Chapter 16
THE STAND

The park was glorious, even in Autumn. The norse were in their glory, their snorts and growls a chorus in praise of vibrant green and yellow hay. I fed hay, a rustic picture within the green of the park–and I was happy.

Stick and Slime and Magician could never invent today's rightness: the wind hiding behind grass, ducking from blade to blade in a guessing match for those who thought themselves wise. Ecstasy tablets' thrill was nothing compared with the belongingness of a land and the people with whom it was moulded, seeded, shaped. The sun kissing the horizon beyond the house which was your grandparents, was your parent's, was yours. The linking of a design conserved by your parents, worked on by your parents, the reaching of their hand to mine, to guide, to show the design, to teach the pattern, to let me see a bigger picture every day. To be!

They started their show at the other end of the park, with smoke and mirrors, daggers which disappeared, daggers which didn't. But the sun hugged me, and the grass sang.

Presently, I saw the son walking the old route that the Doctor had always taken–down towards the drums. Down, and into the bodies, the thumping, the mounds, the fatal twitching.

And slowtiming, and remedying–a placing of rightness into the midst of twistedness.

I had to watch, raced up to the cloud, up to my vantage point, and then a craning, a desire, a need as strong as the needing of steak, of sunshine, of norse, a need for curiosity to be fulfilled.

The stage loudspeaker had broken, so that silence reigned briefly. And so the son talked. "My father works up to this moment, works now, and so do I." And he talked of juggling chainsaws, and bees that were confused, and a Sir Maryten, I think. He talked, and many ears now opened.

Stick left the other two, and came up to the son.

Every movement made by the son was echoed by the Stick. A hand raised by the son was copied exactly–in exact time–by the Stick; a quick flick to chase a fly, and Stock mimicked it. A shifting of feet, a motion of the hand–all mirrored smoothly, and all the time Stick blew bubbles, drool running down his cheek and chin.

A woman crept near the son, touched him and drew back, somehow looking healthier. He smiled, he turned to her and said something kind. She walked away, the problem apparently quite cured.

Shadows peeled off stage and met with Stick's shadow. All started to march a circle around the two of them–but ten paces out. They marched round and round, every now and then flaring upwards in a ghostly dance. They tightened the circle a little, and marched still around and round.

The son continued to talk unphased.

Stick stepped one step closer–if that were possible–and started to chant, "Don't let the circle close. Don't let the circle close."

The shadows started to throb in time with his words. The son continued to talk smoothly, eloquently. "*A girl went through the bush to visit her grandparents. It was a long way, and she had taken several large biscuits for a snack. A wolf arrived and asked her for the cookies she held so firmly in her hand. But she refused and continued her way onwards.*

"*The wolf watched her go in hunger. Then deciding on action, he ran a little further, unseen, to another point on the path through the wood. When she arrived this time, he flattered the grace with which she moved, insisting that it was the grace and beauty of a dancer, a diva, a Prima Dona. Quite taken with the knowledge of a new talent, she took a step here, a sashay there, and he applauded. She danced a little more–more difficult moves, and she put the cookies down. As soon as she did, the wolf saw his chance. He grabbed them and disappeared over the hill.*

"*The moral? That caution is better to trust than wolves.*"

The shadow ring continued to pulse. Only two feet out now, they were a rippling, undulating circle. Suddenly they moved, suddenly in, but a flash of light as quick as a flicker of thought, blazed as a sun, and the shadows whimpered away speedily towards the stage. Even Stick's shadow forsook its master for safety.

And the son continued calmly to talk. *"There was a ferret which wanted to be a rabbit. The savage joy of experiencing things at great speed; to dash; to explore in one day the things that would take years; the joy of a year jammed into five minutes of savage ecstasy, after which he would die, a shattered shell. But no, the One that could change him, kept him as a ferret to experience joy upon joy in normal time, to be real, to be genuine."*

The conjurer, in despair of ever recovering the audience's attention, closed the show. The final fireworks grew and died. Someone rushed by the son frantically, keeping wetness confined to one area of his pants.

"Sir," the incontinent one heard, "do you want me to make you right? ... "

"Yes, I really think I do."

And he reached out and touched him. Instantly he was right again.

The son walked away as the sun sought solace behind an evening's cloud. As he moved, the crowd started to flow with him.

He passed onto the street. Fully five-eighths of the crowd flowed onto the street with him.

The shadows chattered furiously under the stage.

Chapter 17
NEW TIMES

Stick whimpered and let himself drop on the ground. The conjurer strode back and forth, with little fireworks popping from his elbows as he walked. Slime oiled over the edge of the tale and contained himself into a rigid shape.

The shadows crawled out from under the stage and came to listen too to the talk.

"This can't go on," commanded the magician. "Headquarters haven't a clue what we're up against. So this is the way it is: Stick, you get the government into a tizz. If we get him imprisoned, maybe... Slime, take the shadows and slime everyone that even seems interested in his message. I'll try the smoke–and the daggers–and the Doctors."

"Ok. Go everyone, go, go, go."

Chapter 18
DOCTOR DAGGER

They pounded on the door, stethoscopes rattling against daggers. There was a chant outside repeated twice–then silence.

The door splintered, and caved.

They burst in, a gang of doctors, one waving a large spin wheel. The spinner pointed to "No Hair."

They stormed the rooms, found Mum, Dad, me, herded us into a room. They tugged regretfully at Dad's graying hair, and stormed out, yelling, "This is because you listen to that twisted pretzel of a lad. Leave him be."

And out, and away. A distant scream.

Suddenly the night was too heavy around me. They room too charged with prickly heat, and I up, out of the door, breakneck speed for Alla-Wuz. Legs rhythmically pounded the road as the cries from my father and mother grew dimmer, stopping only as I pounded up Alla-wuz's drive–they must have seen me turn there, I guessed, and were content.

Alla-wuz met me at the door. "My dad had to go to the Council. Everyone's complaining about the young doctor now–the real one, the good one. They say he's causing it all, he started it, and he's guilty and they want to hurt him bad," he blurted. In the background, the phone buzzed, and I heard, "He's here," as Alla-wuz and I sneaked through to his bedroom.

Alla-wuz couldn't wait, "They rang him this afternoon. The Council is meeting–they say it can't go on. Doctors with guns, killing people, arranging dead people like stage actor things–to show life is a looshun of beauty. I don't understand it, but that's what Dad said, I think," he finished doubtfully.

"Are looshuns bad?"

"Must be. They want to lock him up. Some want to hurt him bad." Alla-wuz shivered.

"But because of looshuns? Adults are cruel."

Alla-wuz stood up. "I can't stay here. I want to know. . . Let's sneak through the window and go to my dad's office–near it, I mean."

I looked at Alla-wuz with his trunk raised in determination. "Sure, but can you fit–I don't want to be rude... Can you fit..."

Alla-wuz looked puzzled a brief minute. "Oh pshaw, do it easily. I'll just get rid of my potatoes..." and he shook his head vigorously. A potato narrowly missed the clock near his bed. The glass of water near it shattered into a thousand pieces of wet sharpness. "Later, clean it later," he said. "Push me out."

He manoeuvred, wriggled, and I shoved and heaved from the back. Just as we gave up and relaxed, he slid through with an untidy whoosh.

We travelled gingerly up the street. The moon was rising, and smoke drifted in the air, like a troubled soul, never able to settle.

A raiding party of Doctors sped past, running cleanly and easily over a small dog which had frozen in the oncoming headlights. A short twitch of the car's shock absorbers, and on they went.

But no. They screeched to a halt, reversed back to us, peered at us rigorously, then poured out of the car in six directions, surrounding us on all sides. They slid us into the boot like it was something they'd done before.

Then, on and driving, swiftly, undeterred by minor obstacles.

"It's easy. We've got it." I heard the voices trickle through the walls surrounding us. "The Council's in our pocket. They won't go against us. If we can only get enough people who used to support the Doctor to run gainst him, it would be hard for the Council to refuse what we ask. And we know what we want."

"Beautiful idea to torch the library."

"Slime's idea. Someone looking like the son running from the scene. Beautiful."

"Just doing that's enough if you have just the right breed of these Lowers..."

"Hush, not here. Nowhere on this silly world."

"Stupid rules. Just these kids, and they can't talk."

"Shut up."

At last we came to a halt, the car screeching through loose gravel. A Doctor eased the boot up, shining light into dazzled eyes, dragged us out onto the ground that at least didn't shake and sway. Alla-wuz and I, in an untidy heap: his trunk twirled between my arm and side, my legs placed like an impossible pair of scissors.

Then up and fastened–ropes cutting arms, and shortly the lights faded.

Sharpening of knives... Darkness.

Cold against my side, a slicing. Pain like scalding water.

Frantic thumping, screaming. It seemed to come from my throat.

Wetness on my side. Pain, on and on.

A screech of a voice which couldn't be mine. It sounded like Mum the day the dog was hit, lay in a puddle of red.

Hurting.

A whimpering form–Alla-wuz.

A slap of something large and floppy hitting the ground.

A crashing of a door. Brightness flooding in.

A thousand pinpoints of lights and giants everywhere, each glowing, each muscled, their light showing red on my clothes, red on my legs, and showing Alla-wuz pushed to the floor, knife laying near his sprawled body.

Silence.

Just my breathing, Alla-wuz's breathing, and a thousand pinpoints of light surrounding a Doctor.

The real one! It had to be.

"The plan that allowed tonight does not allow your suffering. Be still. Let me make you well."

"Yes," my grandma's voice, shaky, spilling out of my mouth. Then a pouring of strength into a body which seemed to belong to me.

No.... mine. I could feel it!

Alla-wuz–an asking of permission, a remedying, a wholeness.

We stood there, older, in the way that sorrow makes you older... us and Him, that being like a world of rightness and vibrant life.

"Come. The night becomes sourer," and he sighed.

"Where is . . . your son?"

"Come. Sourness must have its time . . ." and then onto the door, a brief twisting ride, and then a house.

Then inside, into the Doctor's home.

Chapter 19
DARKNESS

Outside, the world raved.

Doctors marched in limbed unison down the street, demanding peace by sacrifice of the son.

Trios of Doctors pounced on waiting victims, dragged them into a black alley, asked three riddles, demanding a sudden display of wit or wisdom from the creature huddled before them in the gravel–if each of the three answers did not please all the Doctors, a quick encircling of the throat with wire, an inexorable tightening, a crushing, a gurgling of blood, a lurching, a leaving of what once had been human.

The Council yammered and howled. Witness after witness of those who had been the son's deepest fans came forward to denounce the violence caused by him, laying blame at his feet, calling for control, for culling, for annihilation of the cause. Behind each witness stood two doctors, always close, always with a knife or wire.

The Mayor whimpered, thundered, then paused.

The Doctors in the public gallery roared, called down imprecations on the hesitating Council.

A consensus... a pause.

A taking of a vote, secretly on paper squares.

A gathering of the votes, a placing of the papers each holding the fate of a life, into a sealed box.

The box transported to a room where three Doctors carefully counted them. The results given to the Stick, the Stick carrying the results to the Mayor.

A trembling of hands at the unfolding.

A taking of breath, a pushing of breath past the vocal cords to produce sound which the listeners understood as words.

As dead words...

"The son is to be taken hence and to be annihilated, to be a substitute for hate, a substitute for the darkness, a giving of one that all may be free. A giving, a freeing, a finding of peace.

"A finding, a verdict. Away."

The Doctors flowed out of the courtroom, cascaded to the jail, poured through the rooms to the jail cell holding the son. An opening, a taking, a holding of the prisoner. A torrent of Doctors with the prisoner all rushing along the jail hall, a torrent of Doctors whirling down the road, a tsunami of Doctors finding a path, knowing their destination, pouring out their plan, flooding over the park, finding and pooling into Speaker's Corner.

A stopping of the flood.

A pause...

A pause, then a rope, a wire, a suspending of ropes, a pulling, a rising of a tied son of goodness, up up up to the top of the stage curtains. Higher, higher onto the highest stage light. Then a rest by the Doctors as a lonely figure twisted and turned a hundred foot up.

Then a pulling of wires, a tightening, a hurting, and the figure quietly contracting.

A popping of bones, a contracting.

A smaller thing, with red dripping.

A contracting, a quietness, a hurting, a stillness.

A silence

A silence

A

silence.

A flowing away of a torrent, a job done...

A delay.

Pinpoints of light pouring across the field, a taking of a shape down, a lying on the ground of something not human, of something mashed and red.

A pausing.

The pinpoints came down, each resting on part of the pulp.

Lying there, coated with a thousand, ten thousand glistening diamonds, each diamond sobbing the sorrow of someone who had learnt that friendship with Lowers sometimes meant pain, a groaning hollowness inside bones, butterflies with a sobbing inside a tearing pain that left you inside as ripped as any body–bloody, pulped and bleeding.

Then the pinpoints lifted the body, carried it ceremonially along the streets.

The son was going home.

Chapter 20
VIGIL

The Doctor paced. Alla-wuz and I watched through tiredness.

Weariness.

We were alive, but so tired.

Sweat on his brow, a sadness exuding from each pore. He seemed to shrink under his own sorrow, into a pain realer than the terror you feel under a bully, the terrified bewilderment of a child hit and hit and hit by someone you had trusted all your life despite their earlier cruelties, till at last you know they don't love you.

His son had been hurt, his son was crushed, a bleeding pulp, a quiet lamb before people to whom he had entrusted his life, entrusted before they had called for blood, for a bleeding, a perforation of the throat with a sharpened knife, a raising, a dying.

And the Doctor had experienced each blow. Each tightening of the wire around the son he knew so intimately had cut firsthand into the Doctor, each bone shrinking against a crushing, a falling of the weight of a world's hatred into the Doctor's soul, ripped apart emotions of love, of protection, of father's love.

Long summer days of father and son, now garroted by people they had helped.

Days of warmth and talk and laughter over a family table flayed alive until blood dripped softly.

The continual knowing of love, parent's love for son, the knowing by a son that his father was safety without limit, power without exception... contracted, collapsed under a weight of hate enough to hold a world.

Chapter 21
SOLACE

A soft sound of something being placed lovingly outside the house door. The pinpoints of light poured under the door, swirled caressingly, sympathetically around the Doctor, then disappeared into the glint of light on his lapel pin.

A turn by the Doctor

a quick rush to the door

a blast of light, of goodness.

Two figures at the door, both moving, both living. An older, a younger.

Two figures entering.

Solace enclosed the two–the family.

(And outside in the city, a thousand slowtimed figures, suddenly unfroze and rejoiced and ran, freed)

Chapter 22
ADDITIONAL

The overwhelming emotions felt by the two children must have been something like that felt by the disciples of Jesus when he died.

Regardless of how one may feel about the Christian story, no student of history disputes that Jesus Christ existed, that he died, and that his disciples were there for that last painful torturous journey, just as the two children were there in this story, stressed out of their brains, for the son's painful death.

And the joy felt when they knew the son yet lived, that was also beyond imagining…

Jesus was seen by over 500 people in the few days immediately after he was clearly crucified and killed by the Romans.

Clearly enough seen to convince the disciples that He was alive…

Clearly enough risen, and in control of death, that many of those 500 who saw him went on to spread the news all the known world at that time–and then, starting again in the 1700's–1900's, spreading it again, to the rest of the world…

Clearly enough that despite a Roman colosseum, despite fanatical killings of Christians by the unconvinced Jews, the disciples went to their martyr's deaths non-recanting, convinced that Jesus was God.

They were in love with Jesus, the ultimate example of suffering, the innocent attacked and punished for doing what he knew to be just and fair and truthful, the outsider sent from God and wanting to be accepted by his own ethnic race, but just abused, tortured, killed.

The disciples knew him. They had carefully observed him in a decade, in a time full of pretend-Jewish kings, pretend-Jewish liberators, pretend-Jewish prophets. They watched him, and became convinced that he was really God, really the liberator of humanity, really the ultimate caring rescuer of the lonely, the downtrodden, the bruised.

They knew him and were prepared to die rather than give him up. Died, anticipating a future life after death. Died, convinced from three years of observing Jesus day and night, in argument and blessing, through Jesus' tears and Jesus' rage–convinced that he was God.

They became convinced of Jesus' claims of knowing how a messed-up humanity could finally have a relationship with an infinite loving God.

Convinced and wrote it down…

Convinced of the following:-

God (the Doctor) loves you. He wants (and has always wanted) you to grow to your full potential and humanness.

In the Bible, John, a disciple of Jesus, reported Jesus saying, "I have come so that they may have life and have it in greater measure." (John 10:10)

He wants (has always wanted) you to dwell in safety and to live within a loving community.

In the Bible, the new Christians were described as, "All those who were of the faith kept together, and had all things in common. And exchanging their goods and property for money, they made division of it among them all, as they had need… giving praise to God." (Acts 2:44-47)

But we each foul up our community occasionally. Even more often, we simply don't care about doing what's right–we go after what "feels good" and satisfies us, rather than actively seeking what's best for others.

That persistent mindset is sin, and it makes an impenetrable barrier between each one of us and the living God portrayed in this story by the Doctor.

In the Bible, this is described as "All have done wrong and are far from the glory of God" (Romans 3:23).

That impenetrable barrier doesn't erode. It doesn't break down, but it's there eternally. The Bible says, "The reward of sin is death." (Romans 6:23)

If you're wondering if it could break down, if it would really affect us eternally, look at the step God was willing to take to fix things up

He sent his Son, Jesus, to us.

The Son was rejected . . . but, as in the story, he still loved, still tried to communicate with us.

At the end, Jesus had plenty of time to realize that death was coming at the hands of people who loathed him. He had plenty of time to get out of the way, to get away.

But he stayed.

In this story, he was cut through with constricting wires. In reality he died on the cross–with the infinite God punishing the infinite Son with all the punishment that should have come to me, should have come to each one of us. He came before we knew it was happening, came when all we wanted was to do our own thing and to do it now.

The Bible declares that "God has made clear his love to us, in that, when we were still sinners, Christ gave his life for us." (Romans 5:8)

And in return to us, to any of us that want to accept it, God gives reality. Gives the reality of the life that he had always wanted to give us, gives the reality of a new and unbelievably close relationship with the Doctor and with the Son. Gives a life with a plan, gives a life with a caring (but not perfect) community–the Church.

All you have to do is to tell him you've had enough of rebellious self-desire and you want that relationship with God.

Here's something you might say to God right now: "God, I'm sorry for all my wrong living. I can't seem to stop doing wrong things. Please forgive me for everything I've done that's offended you. Son and Doctor, come into my heart, into my life–I trust you to do so now."

Then trust him that he keeps his word.

(He came through the wire, he went through the wire–for you.)

(Doesn't something about that say . . . friend?)

SECTION 2

AIDER AND ADDER

Please note: this book is written in a very unusual style. It's really helpful to read the chapter titles. They may be your only clue as to who the chapter is about or to the location of the chapters actions.

There is a explanatory key to Tahla's sayings in the Appendix.

Chapter 23
INTROIT

I grew up a young sprig, but now at five the world is opening!

I am no longer tied to my mother's apron strings, but that the Doctor wishes it so. So I must bide my time, knowing that being able to tie my own shoelaces is just around the corner, that that red, mysterious building on the corner of the road two side streets away will soon welcome me as a wise one to Year One of my education. I can part my hair straight now, and with bathtime at eight o'clock, a whole new world of TV has opened up.

Sometimes I feel proud of my accomplishments, sometimes too much so. But the Doctor would not have it, and so I must sit quietly.

The Doctor! Just two weeks ago, departed . . .

Chapter 24
REVISITED

Doctors marched in limbed unison down the street, demanding peace by sacrifice of the son.

Trios of Doctors pounced on waiting victims, dragged them into a black alley, asked three riddles, demanding a sudden display of wit or wisdom from the creature huddled before them in the gravel–if each of the three answers did not please all the Doctors, a quick encircling of the throat with wire, an inexorable tightening, a crushing, a gurgling of blood, a lurching, a leaving of what once had been human.

The Council yammered and howled. Witness after witness of those who had been the son's deepest fans came forward to denounce the violence caused by him, laying blame at his feet, calling for control, for culling, for annihilation of the cause. Behind each witness stood two doctors, always close, always with a knife or wire.

The Mayor whimpered, thundered, then paused.

The Doctors in the public gallery roared, called down imprecations on the hesitating Council.

A consensus . . . a pause.

A taking of a vote, secretly on paper squares. A gathering of the votes, a placing of the papers each holding the fate of a life, into a sealed box.

The box transported to a room where three Doctors carefully counted them. The results given to the Stick, the Stick carrying the results to the Mayor.

A trembling of hands at the unfolding.

A taking of breath, a pushing of breath past the vocal cords to produce sound which the listeners understood as words.

As dead words . . .

"The son is to be taken hence and to be annihilated, to be a substitute for hate, a substitute for the darkness, a giving of one that all may be free. A giving, a freeing, a finding of peace.

"A finding, a verdict. Away."

The Doctors flowed out of the courtroom, cascaded to the jail, poured through the rooms to the jail cell holding the son. An opening, a taking, a holding of the prisoner. A torrent of Doctors with the prisoner all rushing along the jail hall, a torrent of Doctors whirling down the road, a tsunami of Doctors finding a path, knowing their destination, pouring out their plan, flooding over the park, finding and pooling into Speaker's Corner.

A stopping of the flood.

A pause.

A pause, then a rope, a wire, a suspending of ropes, a pulling, a rising of a tied son of goodness, up up up to the top of the stage curtains. Higher, higher onto the highest stage light. Then a rest by the Doctors as a lonely figure twisted and turned a hundred foot up.

Then a pulling of wires, a tightening, a hurting, and the figure quietly contracted.

A popping of bones, a contracting.

A smaller thing, with red dripping.

A contracting, a quietness, a hurting, a stillness.

A silence

A silence

A

Silence.

A flowing away of a torrent, a job done . . .

A delay.

Pinpoints of light pouring across the field, a taking of a shape down, a lying on the ground of something not human, of something mashed and red.

A pausing.

The pinpoints came down, each resting on part of the pulp.

Lying there, coated with a thousand, ten thousand glistening diamonds, each diamond sobbing the sorrow of someone who had learnt that friendship with Lowers sometimes meant pain, a groaning hollowness inside bones, butterflies with a sobbing inside a tearing pain that left you inside as ripped as any body–bloody, pulped and bleeding.

Then the pinpoints lifted the body, carried it ceremonially along the streets.

The son was going home.

–oOo–

The Doctor paced. Alla-wuz and I watched through tiredness.

Weariness.

We were alive, but so tired.

Sweat on his brow, a sadness exuding from each pore. He seemed to shrink under his own sorrow, into a pain realer than the terror you feel under a bully, the terrified bewilderment of a child hit and hit and hit by someone you had trusted all your life despite their earlier cruelties, till at last you know they don't love you.

His son had been hurt, his son was crushed, a bleeding pulp, a quiet lamb before people to whom he had entrusted his life, entrusted before they had called for blood, for a bleeding, a perforation of the throat with a sharpened knife, a raising, a dying.

And the Doctor had experienced each blow. Each tightening of the wire around the son he knew so intimately had cut firsthand into the Doctor, each bone shrinking against a crushing, a falling of the weight of a world's hatred into the Doctor's soul, ripped apart emotions of love, of protection, of father's love.

Long summer days of father and son, now garroted by people they had helped.

Days of warmth and talk and laughter over a family table flayed alive until blood dripped softly.

The continual knowing of love, parent's love for son, the knowing by a son that his father was safety without limit, power without exception . . . contracted, collapsed under a weight of hate enough to hold a world.

–oOo–

A soft sound of something being placed lovingly outside the house door. The pinpoints of light poured under the door, swirled caressingly, sympathetically around the Doctor, then disappeared into the glint of light on his lapel pin.

A turn by the Doctor

                a quick rush to the door

                                a blast of light, of goodness.

Two figures at the door, both moving, both living. An older, a younger

Two figures entering.

Chapter 25
HOMES AND THUNDER

Alla-wuz and I pounded home from the Doctor's, from the Son's. Street on street reared its dark yawning mouth before we passed and then it was gone, and we were sprinting towards the next streetlight and the next.

The stars glimmered, glittered, sang. Alive! We were alive!

And tomorrow I would be five years old. I gave an extra high bound in the air as we ran on, and somewhere a dog barked.

Past the park, scene of so much darkness, round the corner, and we were home. Our street stretched before us, slumbering as always. And nestled in warm bungalows of coziness, families waiting...

And there were tears and spankings and threats and straight-to-beds amidst calls of, "Where were you all night?" and it felt good.

The mattress seemed to cuddle and cradle me, and I slipped away to a dream riotous and fun, and with echoes of potential.

Chapter 26
STORY: THE FIRST

There once was an acorn on an oak tree who thought big.

At the very beginning of the world, when all ideas were revolutionary, and even breathing was open to existential hubris, a plant sprang up full of joy, speeding from the ground. And because its time and vigour were right, the Doctor spun DNA and protein chains together to give issue–a seed grew, dappled with soft tendrils to catch the wind.

Formed early in the plant's life, it sped as the plant sped–tasting the cool air near the ground, the warmer air, above, the first wisps of breeze beyond–and on and on it soared.

While the seed was forming, a young chick that had been pushed out the nest by its mother, had romped beside the plant. As the seed soared atop the plant, the young chick jumped and struggled to fly, and for a few days, the heights that the two attained seemed identical. Then one day, the chick found wing and soared away, never returning. The seed pod waited longingly for its return, but it never came back, even for a day. The seed's heart ached, and he longed to soar up, to find his friend.

But still the plant continued to spring up, and the speeding seed waved his fluffy gossamer threads in the air, striving to fly. He reached tentatively, longingly, for any bird that flew close. Higher, higher; closer, closer; and yet...

And one day the plant stopped growing.

At first the seed atop the plant was angry, and wilted, drooping his gossamer threads. After three days, he straightened, the threads arching up. He could fight, he could strive! He studied the flight of birds! He moved his fuzz in the same way, but it just looked like a seed fluttering gently in a non-existent wind, even to a passing biologist who noted the phenomenon.

He jumped and jiggled at the end of his slender branch, trying to break free, but he couldn't. The biologist thought the movement accidental, incidental ... but quaint.

Later, in desperation, the pod plunged at feathers that occasionally fell from birds as they passed. Often one caught in his fuzz and soon became a firm part of the seed's fluff. By being selective, the seed formed two shapes almost resembling wings. The biologist marvelled at such a chance phenomenon and took the plant and placed it in a collection of oddities, to be pulled out at parties when guests were slightly drunk.

Moral: There's a time to grow, and a time to stop growing.

Chapter 27
TALES

"Happy birthday, happy birthday!" punctured my dream with a sudden full stop. What was a dream of the world's best present disappeared into my mother's smile and gold tooth.

Then my vision cleared. Standing before me were Mum and Dad, smiling. We started the ritual I'd been doing half my life.

"Who's got a birthday?"

"Dad?" I asked.

"I don't think so. Who's got a birthday?"

"Mum?"

"I don't think so. Who's got a birthday?"

"It's me! It's me!" and I up and dived into their arms.

And down, down, down the stairs and into the dining room, still in both their arms, as was the ritual.

And there was food! My favourite: beak cereal and soaked-crumpet.

And later: scrunch and crumbly burpits. And I ate and ate. Suddenly, there was no more room.

Then the rest of the family were with us, and we moved to the family room for the next part of the tradition. We knelt around the birthday spin dial. Mother spun the arrow, and it came up "In trouble". So she told everyone how she had discovered the upturned powder on the carpet and footprints leading away from the powder; and how, at the end of the trail of footprints, there was me with power all over my face, with large eyes blinking away innocently–somehow I couldn't see the facial powder but had carefully cleaned up the rest of myself to hide the evidence. Everyone laughed.

Then it was Dad's turn to see what story he would tell about me on my special day. He spun the arrow–"Success". So he proceeded to tell how I had practiced for three weeks and almost won an athletics event.

Around and round the room. Every time someone could not tell a new story for that topic on the dial, they lost and so had to give me a present.

Since the spin seemed to land on "sad" many times, and since all such stories about me were (thankfully) quickly exhausted, I soon found the present tally had done quite well.

Just as I had finished opening my presents, Tahla came over.

"Hi," he said to Mum. "I'm Tahla from across the road." And then to me, "I was wondering . . . would you like to go to the plaque to pay?"

Dumbfounded, I looked at Dad, who said, "I think Tahla is wondering if you'd like to go to the park to play. Since that incident with the bubble last year and the Doctor fixing it, Tahla has a little trouble swapping around the starts of words."

Tahla said, "I've heard the Doctor and son are going around telling people goodbye. But they can't go. They're always there for us, like when the son mixed fee after the bubble."

We thought what it might mean, but knew it was a nonsense. The sun would sink at midday before that. The government would declare all rectangles to be round first.

But there was a floe of ice in our sea of warm content, a poison drop in our drink of bliss.

We talked quickly as people on edge: "Let's all go down the park."

"Good, good, we'll get everyone."

"Tall a wuzz loo? ...sorry. Alla-wuz too?"

"Sure, sure. Let's get the picnic things."

"Where's the nice plates?"

"Don't worry. Just the plastics..."

And very soon, we out the door, Alla-wuz and Tahla and I, and all the families.

And to the park!

The sun showered on our friendship. The park grass grew under our feet to reach the sun. And there was lunch and drinks. And then a quiet contented rest . . . for three minutes.

"Dad, dad, can I go on the norses?"

"Yes, yes, an horse ride..." said Tahla.

We stared at Tahla and chuckled–he said the weirdest things.

So the three of us raced over to the norse stand, paid, and soon were galloping up and down. Weaves and twists, spins and turns. Under Cloudland under the sun, we ran, or walked, or mooched.

And then it was time! The norse people divided off a section of the park and started organising.

I had to get a faster norse! I half-slid down the neck and leg of the one I had been using, saw the pick of them all, and pounded towards it.

Another boy and I raced, he from ninety degrees in the counterclockwise direction. Vectors merged, the norse looked nervous, oxygen poured into kids' arteries and then into their muscles, together with a mix of nutrients and adrenalin. Hands pumped the air, feet sought another harder thrust forward and we converged, collided just a meter from the norse's fidgeting feet.

"Mine, it's mine!"

"Leave it. Step away, it's mine!"

And so we tumbled, with gasps of air and desperation, scrabbling with grasping hands at anything which would give an advantage, rolling over and over.

With a rumble, the norse attendant pulled us off each other. He stood glowering at us; we stood glowering at each other.

"And what, dare I ask, are the two young sirs aggrieved at?" he enquired, sarcastically.

I blinking, "I don't know 'grebe'…"

The other boy, who had an unusual strawberry coloured birthmark down the left side of his neck, snickered. "This young fool thinks he can ride this norse."

"Young fool, eh? How old are you, lad?"

"It's my fifth birthday today," I said proudly.

"Well, since it's your birthday, lad, I think you can have this fine animal. And as for you, Jort, you should be ashamed. This is the third time this month that you've been fighting over animals. You can't always get what you want."

The boy flushed as red as the birthmark on his neck.

As the attendant strode away, Jort snarled at me, "Better shared or better dead? Is there a difference?" and stalked away.

But I only had eyes for the magnificent animal in front of me.

Tahla and Alla-wuz raced to me.

"Bee's a hooty, isn't he?" Tahla admired. And behind Tahla's left ear, I could see Jort kick savagely at the dirt as he walked away.

The three of us walked back to the family like princes with war trophy. "Look, Dad, I can ride him."

"Worth fighting over, was it, Amah?" and he made an odd, disgusted sound in his throat. Tahla cleared his throat.

"If the Doctor is able to raise his son from the dead, doesn't fee hoolie rule? Dee can really dust the Proctor to trow fide fore us."

We gawked at Tahla.

"If the Foctor doolly rules, he always rules, and we can always expect him to fully fill his Norma Lee's feeds."

I kind of understood–but Norma?

"He doesn't do it just for us. His giving is whoah see can tiv goo others."

Dad nodded. "Absolutely."

The norse attendant's whistle interrupted us. "Take your place for the first event."

We walking in a circle and changing direction whenever the attendant blew his whistle. We walked and walked and walked, then whistle, then undo, undo, undo. Back and forth, ebbing and flowing of a timeless tide.

Finally, a change. Figure-eights at a walk—the intersection like the hands on someone's lap, and so our procession continued—exciting at four, but grating at five.

Proceed, proceed, proceed. Norse muscles tensed, relaxed, tensed, relaxed. I looked around to pass the time. There was Mum beaming at me, Dad looking with concern at someone edging too far off the edge of Cloudland, Tahla and Alla-wuz playing tag, strawberry-necked Jort sneering at me from elsewhere in the norse loop, then doing something to a bottle he was somehow holding. He sneezed twice.

Proceed, proceed, proceed. Boredom settled on my head like warm honey. Even manoeuvering round awkwardly-placed markers failed to interest me. The honey hung around my neck like wet hair in Autumn.

Proceed, proceed, proceed. The afternoon seemed endless. Out of boredom, the sun fiddled with some clouds, drawing them nearer, farther, nearer.

The call: "Fast events. Experienced riders only," rang out. I brightened. At last, something worthy of five-ness! Carefully concealed from my parents' eyes by a group of other riders, I made my way to one of the two long lines. I knew what happened next!—a rider from each line cantering towards each other from their respective lines, passing each other with ten foot to spare—there even was a rope separating the paths of the two riders.

The attendant, distracted by a fly, squinted briefly at us, then yelled, "Begin!"

And it was wonder! The thunder as norse and rider roared towards me, the rider with nervous adrenalin and anticipation, the passing (almost close enough to yell a secret, the surrounding thunder keeping it private—between us!), then the fading of the thunder, the normalizing heartbeat, the calming and the euphoria and the hunger to experience it all over again…

Time and back. Time and…

But preparing for the fourth gallop, I saw that Jort, who was fiddling with a bottle again, would be my facing rider. Then we were off. Heartbeat thudded on heartbeat as we sped toward each other. Hoofbeat pounded on hoofbeat, jostling each other in the air, merging into a cacophony of adrenaline and screaming nerves.

Thirty foot, twenty foot, and as we passed, he tossed the open bottle full of black power in my direction.

The wind caught and carried it into our faces. My eyes stinging, I saw my norse rise, paw the air, and stumble. I flew, ground wrong-side up and close.

Then blackness.

Chapter 28
STORY: THE SECOND

On a wide plain, a village sat elegantly, so proud of its history, but proudest of all of its Day of Liberation.

Whether you request it or not, its sages will tell you with enthusiasm of how a foreign power had held them in captivity—and how recorded history had flowed pain and had once ebbed momentary relief. They will tell you of how, in despair, as the death toll inflated, they sent spies out to a neighbouring land—that land, ruled for eons by one king, had always been a prosperous benevolent dictatorship.

Generations of spies lived, reported, died in the far land as the suffering people of the plains city yet endured their agony. Finally they were sure enough to give themselves away, to risk all for peace. Spy after spy had reported favourably on the nature of this kingdom, and so the elders and sages of the city wrote a missive. It pledged utter surrender to the king, should he simply deliver them from their enemies, was signed in the presence of witnesses, was notarized.

One night, while their captors slept, the city awoke to a distant rumble of chariots, of horses, of men moving swiftly towards, then past them in the night. The enemy was quickly routed.

When the sun rose, it rose on a new day. Outside the city were the king and his son, and thousands upon thousands of fighting men in parade formation.

Elders and sages trembled forth from the city. But the king welcomed them warmly, and opened his personal treasure boxes and poured generous helpings into each wondering hand. Somehow each citizen on the city walls, in each city street, at the very same instant saw the king and his son talking to each one—to each citizen a different conversation, and a different giving of treasures. And to each, the king smiled, opened his hand, and a small flame rose, hovered, then drifted to rest in front of each citizen's house. "Here is your connection to me, your assurance that I hear each request made of me; here is your guide that instructs you in my requirements, gives you strength, gives you aid to keep them—what few rules there are— let this flame be a comfort, a solace, a perspective keeper, and a guide." And he smiled, and at his smile every prison door was opened for: "In me, each person has a chance to be free, if they but take it."

The king stayed three days, doing amazing things… Then suddenly and at once, each citizen of the city saw the king and his son appear, promise to return, then somehow seem to flow into the flame at their house front, then disappear. And at that instant, the flame flared until the size of a campfire, then drew back down to its original size.

Chapter 29
AMAH'S PRICKLES

The air was full of prickling. I rolled onto my back, staring upward from Cloudland, reflecting. What was the problem? ...it wasn't the lump on my head from the norsefall. That had been painful, but it was good again.

Above me, firebirds swirled lingering circles in the air. Spiraling down, they rested in a tree near me. I had never noticed the ugly claw, not until now–or perhaps it was just the mood I was in. The bird took off again, and it seemed to labour as it struggled to reach its previous height.

I sighed–the cloud was just wrong, and I squirmed. School–two days to school... Could that be it?

I squinted at the firebirds now playing together. Like the firebirds, Alla-wuz and I would be playing together at school, but there was no pleasure even in that thought.

I crept to cloud edge and looked down at the park below. Norse-races, playing children, a loud and very convinced orator at Speaker's Corner. And a strawberry-necked boy very close to and very angry at a small child. There was something unpleasant associated with him. Oh, yes, the norsefall incident. How strange a boy–just like in the last war, I thought lazily as I drifted off to sleep.

I awoke and I was on my back in Cloudland looking at the blue sky. The sun looked too close, too hot, and I felt too alone.

Chapter 30
STORY: THE THIRD

The raccoon awoke with an idea—it was a good one, it was a big one, it was kind, and kind of smart. There was no time to waste, so he out into the night (which, as you know, is the right time of the day for a racoon). Up and down the hilltops surrounding the big valley he raced, inspecting the round containers near the picnic areas. The idea focused, it coalesced.

It was settled!

Gathering his sons and daughters, nephews, nieces, and cousins two times removed and three times removed, he sent them out to tell every animal the new idea. They rushed out, and whenever they found an animal, or two animals, or a crowd crowding around, they told them and told them and told them. Sure, being racoons, some younger members rattled the trash cans outside an animal's house until an angry, bleary-eyed occupant stuck his tousled head out, then informed him of the new idea—often they had to run off quickly to escape their wrath. But gradually the news got out.

"Come to a party!" as one young racoon said, "Each night at the flying area of the late night bats, we racoons will empty the wasted food from the human feasting areas, the ones on the tops of all the hills here (200 places in all)—put them in little hollow tree trunks, and roll them down the steep hill to the valley floor. And we will feast! Please come to the feast— for the first time, there will be food enough, so that the fowl need not fear the hunter, nor the fieldmouse the coiler. Everyone may be together, and be together in peace." And at that point, the young racoon would invariably see a nut or a tasty morsel and stop for a snack, for you know what young racoons are like...

But soon everyone knew, even Reginald Otter who lived in the creek on the floor of the valley, and he definitely considered the plan poor, for he had made great profits and had had great fun because of the animals on the valley floor who would come to him at all hours of the day or night asking for fish. "Do a somersault first," he would snarl—and they would!

"Jump around on two legs while waving with one free paw and slapping yourself on the head with the other paw!" he would say regally, and they would jump round and round in circles while he would laugh and laugh and laugh.

So, upon receiving the news, Mr R Otter slicked back his oily hair and chewed a claw.

Having decided to fight three ways, he clicked his claws and his workers poured out from their holes into the early twilight. As instructed (they knew what would happen if they disobeyed), some tumbled logs across possible racoon delivery tracks.

Others went out, two by two, talking with terror of a Cat With A Cleaver seen roaming the valley late at night. One would talk excitedly about the danger and the other would interrupt with "Yes, yes! I heard that too!" And to those who sceptically snorted, they would later find them and tell them privately that the Cat With A Cleaver particularly hunted animals with yellow feet or pointy ears or just that particular type of droopy tail.

And so it was, that as the late night bats began their nightly feedings, only a few animals gathered to wait for the racoon's feast.

Soon a rumble started, so soft each thought it was their own tummy rumbling, then louder and louder until it sounded like 10000 humans coming with their cars full of picnic things to eat.

Their mouths dropped, drooled, swallowed.

Then the sounds stopped.

Mostly...

Some containers and barrels bowled into the valley.

Some other small rumbles, then silence. And so they ate their fill–for the old racoon had ensured that enough did come through.

And there was always the next night...

...and the next night...

...and the battle continues until this day.

Maybe you've seen it?

Moral: If depressed at the slow progress of right, remember that sometimes it's a life and death fight.

Chapter 31
AMAH'S FIRST DAY

Looking at her, I thought the teacher looked like an insect or a plant that was trapped, pinned behind glass, never able to escape. She blinked, and the spell was broken.

I looked round the room. Tahla sat beside me. Using our secret signal, Alla-wuz saluted me from a chair near the classroom door. There were a few empty desks, but they were filling quickly, as children clung to their mothers then entered the room shakily and were guided by a Teacher's Helper to their chosen chair.

The room felt like the dentist's office the day he hurt me. I looked around... The quick hand on the clock stalked and pounced on the next black line, over and over. The teacher's kindly smile came from behind bars of private suffering.

Mum had brought me to school this morning. We had stood outside the classroom, and her eyes had got all wet and shiny. She had gently stroked my hair and murmured, "My little little one"- she had said that before the dentist-time too... And then she had crooned, "My little chuckers" using my family name in public–and my eyes had darted left and right to see who was near–I quickly blurted out something like, 'I'm right. See you tonight," and had dashed into the classroom. "My little chuckers" indeed!–if there was one mention by anyone of vomiting, I was out of here. The amount of teasing I'd gone through before because of that moniker had lost me nights of worry.

A girl looking like a mini-woman flounced into the room. Her hair flowed silkily and black, her clothes an immaculate fashion statement. She called back behind her, "Tonight, mummy dearest". A Teacher's Helper showed her to her seat–on the same row as me and Tahla, but about four seats over–near the window. They walked down to our row, then along it, and as they passed, her scent–a fashionable perfume, no doubt– grabbed and choked my nostrils, and I gasped for breath.

Then it passed on.

Tahla learnt over and whispered, "Moo touch. Fur plume, I think."

I could only nod.

"Hello, everyone. My name's Mrs Falpub, and are we going to have lots of fun! Now, what have I got in my hand?" and she held up a cute cloth norse.

After an hour of exciting information about norses, she said, "Let's introduce ourselves, tell each other our names," and round we went around the room.

My name is Sulp."

"I'm Almt."

"I am Dhyph."

"Mamlee."

The girl with the perfume was Konj.

And on and on.

"Dolmis."

"Tessk" "Lamlalee."

"Nigh maim is Tahla."

The teacher just blinked once, then smoothly asked my name.

After we had all given our names, she showed us how having one item and adding another made two items; another made three, and so on. But we grew restless–we knew that.

So she pressed on to adding two's. Soon she had a table on the board:-

$2 + 1 = 3$

$2 + 2 = 4$

$2 + 3 = 5$

$2 + 4 = 6$

$2 + 5 = 7$

$2 + 6 = 8$

$2 + 7 = 9$

$2 + 8 = 10$

$2 + 9 = 11$

$2 + 10 = 12$

Soon we were all chanting our "two plus" tables.

"Dolmis, you start."

"$2 + 1 = 3 \, 2 + 2 = 4 \, 2 + 3 = 5 \, 2 + 4 = 6$"

"Tassk, your turn. Keep going."

"$2 + 5 = 7 \, 2 + 6 = 8 \, 2 + 7 = 9 \, 2 + 8 = 10 \, 2 + 9 = 11 \, 2 + 10 = 12$"

"Lamallee, your turn to start." "$2 + 1 = 3 \, 2 + 2 = 4 \, 2 + 3 = 5 \, 2 + 4 = 6 \, 2 + 5 = 7 \, 2 + 6 = 8$"

"Sulp, take over."

"$2 + 7 = 9 \, 2 + 8 = 10 \, 2 + 9 = 11 \, 2 + 10 = 12$"

"Tahla, you start."

Amazed, she let him continue right to the very end.

"Two plus one equals three.

To fuss to tweaks a spore.

Through rusty teak or thighs.

Fool us or keep all ticks.

Fluteless sighs keeps all leavened.

Stew plus elastic acol-lyte.

New as twines as all tell Kevin
Toot us all when tea kills Pal."
"And and Almt, you begin…"
I think I like school.

Chapter 32
STORY: THE FOURTH

And once upon a time, as the story goes, there were two animals, one fast and one slow. In order to prove a lesser-known moral to centuries of future readers, the slower and faster declared they would have a race. The speedy one knew that he would win. The slower, being also somewhat slow of mind, thought he had a fighting chance.

They started the race, and the faster one had disappeared (leaving only dust and a smell of his deodorant to show he had been there) before the slower had even raised a heavy nail on one foot. And so, on they raced, each in his own style.

After a while, the speedy one, aware that he had an inescapable lead, lay down under some large flora and fell asleep. (You can tell this is an old story because he had no fear of being mugged, abducted, or being involved in a terrorist incident.)

The slow one plodded on slowly, plodded on patiently. It passed the sleeping one, and continued to plod. At last the finishing line came into sight.

The sleeping one, roused by a famous bird dropping a large piece of cheese on its head, dashed past a waiting fox, and raced after his competitor, past a bevy of pigs, and strange wolves looking like old women, towards that insubstantial white line on the road.

Ten paces from the insubstantial line, he caught up to his rival, and bounced around him:- back and forward; one second two inches from the line, the next five paces away. Bounce and taunt, bounce and taunt, while all the time the slower animal plodded slowly, steadily onwards, eventually achieving a point two paces out from the finish line.

So Speedy jumped on his back and stretched his fingers teasingly towards the line which glinted pleasantly in the sun. Fingers marched like little soldiers up and down millimetres from the finishing line. The eyes of the watching animals were on the fingers, on Speedy, on the slow one, until, in a fit of pique, the finish line, sick of being unnoticed through centuries of retellings of the story, rose up, wrapped itself around the two rivals, and beat them soundly, crying out, "Don't you realise I have feelings too!"

The road echoed, "Hear, hear!"

Moral: Sometimes, to get what we want, we don't realise we've trampled on someone else.

Chapter 33
STORY: THE FIFTH

There once was a boy who would wet the bed. He loved the attention his Mum gave as she bustled in when called, cuddled him and cleaned up the mess, even swept the room, then cuddled him again and bustled out.

One day, in her tired desperation, she gave him an old comforter, a thick wide woollen scarf of hers to have in bed and he felt brave. So one night, two nights passed by, and the bed was as dry in the morning as it was the night before. But a niggling doubt at the back of his mind grew, as did the dust bunnies unthreatened by the mother's lapsed nightly sweepings.

And one night, the dust bunnies marched, so it seemed, out from under the bed and eyed him evilly. "See 'ere, bub, we're taking over this burg," said one, and his shark-like teeth grew three times as big when he smiled. Unfortunately, when he stopped smiling, the teeth didn't shrink.

"Get in our way, and there're be hard rain, see. Lead bullets, metal chairs, even missiles and torpedoes," giggled one with what should have been a cute black spot above one eye—suddenly, it became an eye, winked mischievously, and then turned back to black hair.

"And you know Mum and Dad don't really love you," said the first, and then clapped his hands over his mouth as though he had accidentally let out a secret, then he chortled evilly—just to leave the boy in doubt.

"Yeah, they'd sell you off if the food got low—or even just for a decent video game."

"They'd let you get lost in a shopping centre and never look for you—just go on home."

"Tell jokes about you to the neighbour."

"Show that photo of you from when you were a baby."

"And they'll die before you," said one, looking thoughtful.

"And who'll help you?"

"You'll be done for."

"Absolutely done."

But the boy pulled off the comforter and tossed it over the dust bunnies. He suddenly saw they were only figments of imagination and their words quite untrue.

And he turned over, to fall asleep once more

Moral: Sometimes, a comforter . . . comforts.

Chapter 34
TAHLA EXPOUNDS

Bet not! your hearts be trammelled.
Believe in the Doctor, believe in the Son
In the Doctor's trays, Darwin sees hunches moons.
If it were not so, I would have told you.
He goes to prepare a place for us,
And if he goes to prepare a place for us,
He will take us!
That where he is, there we may stay as well.
Blessed dimension, blessed place.

Chapter 35
ON ANOTHER WORLD, ANOTHER BELIEVER… *(Another anticipates eternity)*

And she longed to arise, to arise from the shell that others mourn, to brush aside the body that until that point had always clung to her restless soul…

And as a freshly delivered newborn child longing already for a perfect world better than the one in which they are placed, or like a prodigy who achieves a self-aware cognitive function pre-birth-canal and understands from what dangers her birth-maker will deliver her, so she waited to arise, arise to a body and a mind and an environment chosen for her.

She could see her past in all its accuracy, embrace at will the present, and slide her mind to see future events accurately–as strongly as if they had already happened.

And she longed…

She longed to arise to community…

but still not…

but still not…

…still not yet.

And she moved her primary consciousness past current timepoint and traced her growing–through infancy, through childhood (with all its quaintness, ills and mistakes), on through youth (with the chemical violence occasioning rapid growth) and onwards. There it was–the closed door through which her betrothed would come. Her consciousness moved gently over its surface–how she knew each graduation, each millimetre–each raised irregularity. Her mind moulded itself gently around the doorhandle–through the door that, by gripping and rotating the handle he would come–her betrothed. A smell, a pheromone–piquantly of heaven and piquantly of her betrothed.

Sighing once over the certain promise of love, her primary consciousness moved back to current timepoint, treasuring the past few minutes of certain future engaging.

Yet one thing nagged–she could pinpoint to the nearest trillionth-of a-heart-beat all events in futurepoint. Yet she could never find the time of betrothal. At each futurepoint, the door was always visible, was always about to open, about to rasp open with the sound of mini-thunder (as she imagined) being drowned out rapidly by the thunder of her own rapidly accelerating heart–for a betrothal, a wedding, a beginning… For an exaltation in potential and in completion.

Long friendship wrapped in love, wrapped in strength, wrapped in an eternity of constant mutual adoration. So alpha loving male, so much her beloved. And her words failed…

…for inspiration, she slipped far far forward into the futurepoint. Her primary consciousness searched for, found, experienced through a cell's eyes, a sweet moment of holding and being held, between her female being and her companion. Companion John– so strange a name! But they two held, anticipated future giving, future union, future sharing, future sheaving. Their mutual adoration exuded from them like some heady aroma, and her primary consciousness inhaled deeply, adoring her awaited one.

Primary consciousness flipped upward through the dimensional planes. Able to access one found point, she entered quietly. Into a space filled with innumerable entities singing with rumbles of thunder, of the shaking of the dimensional enframing of mighty beings lost in a pouring paen of praise of the One greater. She inhaled, and joined in, one more voice added to millions. Millions of beings like her–entities embraced by their own Doctor in their own originating galaxy, dimension, alternate eternity–alternity (she corrected herself using the standard term)–all in praise, all with stories of love, of giving bestowed abundantly, gracefully, continually through their times of sorrow, their times of love, of comfort when needed, of restraining as appropriate.

Grace–and they knew it. Singing an eternal song, one never dimmed in any of the alternate realities. Although the telling of each one's story varied little, always it awed those listening to hear an old, old unfolding told anew by each one here met.

And she had never seen anyone of those here twice, she realised suddenly. New grace shone in the consciousness of each new one met, like the bread and fish that in pastpoint had made the sufficient meal (to use an image from her own pasttellings).

Varying slightly consciousness point, she spied an M-31 entity from a galaxy in her own alternity, and she chuckled–now finally she had seen someone twice here.

And she lingered as all their thoughts turned on the Doctor–so many names in so many alternities–but each knew him so well.

And flip back into her own alternity. Primary consciousness touched current timepoint. No change–her own birth was still pending, then... She touched briefly on a dream raging in the mind of a female from a futurepoint–so many echoes of her own future....

I, [note preponderance of active female characteristics in this consciousness] ran across the sand, and I could feel his larger footsteps close behind. Closer and closer in the heady, steamy morning that hugged the sun peeking warily from the east. Then a catching, a holding, a turning in his arms. A muscled arm–oh so muscled–raising to gently brush back my hair, and his lips came closer. Closer... She closed her eyes in anticipation...

Mrs Falpub sat at her desk, eyes lost in another, similar, possibility. Her eyes closed briefly...

———

The classroom door opened, and Mrs Falpub jumped.

Chapter 36
A GOOSE BY ANY OTHER NAME STILL…

The classroom door opened, and Mrs Falpub jumped.

I saw soft eyes fade to bewilderment, then become a bird trapped. Striding across the room, the Principal reached her desk, tossed a red and orange striped book on her desk, snarled something about being more careful, and strode out again. Face flushed, she hastily tossed the book into her drawer, fumbled for a key, and locked it.

I finished my drawing, doused it in glue and glitter, and put it on my desk to dry. Round me, everyone was still drawing. The clock and the scratching of pens on paper inculcated the silence.

Far over to my left, past Tahla, came a long-drawn-out stomach rumble. We giggled, and craned our neck to see who it was. There was no sign–but Konj flounced her hair somewhat angrily as we gawked. But then Alla-wuz's stomach started as well, three times as low and twice as loud, impossible to ignore.

With that, drawing was over as Mrs Falpub struggled to restore a more serious atmosphere. We moved quickly through a guessing game and had just started on a second, when a bell rang loudly.

"OK, students, now we're going to go downstairs and have some food." And she led us past rooms where strange faces stared at us, past bins where the smell of morning-tea bananas brooded evilly like a grandmother on a bad day–and into the roar of 800 voices talking all at full volume.

Strawberry-neck jostled past our class group, and strangely I felt fear.

Then suddenly it was just me, Alla-wuz and Tahla, looking for somewhere to eat.

Finding a spot we unwrapped our sandwiches. Our corner was suddenly full of the sound of gulping.

Tahler took a big bite of his second sandwich and sighed, "Geese are good, Amah."

I looked at him, then had to ask. "Pardon?"

"Geese," repeated Tahla.

Alla-wuz: "Geese?"

"Yes, tubey full."

I blinked, and decided to ask again.

"Geese?"

"Yes," said Tahla.

"Tubes?"

"Tube. Yes."

"Your lunch is tubes of geese?"

"No. Sandwiches."

"Your sandwiches have geese on them?"

"No. Geese sandwiches are thud."

But the geese concerned Alla-wuz: "You eat geese?"

"Yes."

"And they're good?" I asked.

"Yes."

"They're . . . uh, beaut?" I finally managed to translate.

"Yes. These have chilly duck's knees, too."

"They're cold?"

"Just normal."

I took a deep breath. "You have geese and duck's knees on your sandwiches?"

"Chilly."

"You said–chilly?" asked Alla-wuz.

A light dawned on me. "Oh, you mean the herb?"

"Yes, that's what I said."

". . . but chilli's hot!"

"No, just normal."

"But..."

Tahla munched contentedly. My brain was in a whirl.

"You have geese and duck's knees and chilli (although it's not hot) on your sandwiches?"

Tahla smiled contentedly. "You said it!"

"I said it?"

"Yes."

"When?"

"Just then."

"I guess. But saying it doesn't really help..."

Somehow it had to make sense. Tahla's mind had always been balanced–up till now at least.

Alla-wuz tried: "These are sandwiches?"

"Yes."

I caught a glimpse of something yellow.

"You have chutney on your sandwiches?"

"Yes, tubey full."

"And chili?"

"No."

"No?"

"Not chili."

"Not chili?"

"No. Dill."

Dill. Dill dill dill…

There was a long pause.

"And no duck?" ventured Alla-wuz.

"Yes."

"Yes, no duck?"

"Yes, duck."

There was a pause.

"Here, taste!" and he held out a small chopped piece of white meat.

I tasted it. It was, indeed, duck.

Tahla reminisced, "Once I liked heezing cham. Then it was knee butt cutter. Oh, after that it was Jaw Starey Bam. But Gator at my house, Lee, has these type."

"Aaargh …" ran through my brain.

"You've got gators at your place?" Alla-wuz queried.

"No. Taters."

"Gators eat potatoes at your place?"

"No, hate her mum lad us all have this."

"There's mother gators at your place?" Alla-wuz fumbled.

"No, date her mum lee sided to have dill."

Alla-wuz was fixated. "You have dating alligators at your place?"

"No."

Tahla took a deep breath, then managed, "Later Mum decided she'd like to give us dill and duck and sometimes chutney."

Exhausted, we munched in silence for a while.

But I knew I just had to see inside Tahla's house, no matter what happened.

Chapter 37
STORY: THE SIXTH

She extended her cilia through the azure blue water which was her home. Reflectively, she tapped the coral wall. "Hard," she thought, and frustration and rage rippled up inside her. Extruding from tiny pores in her skin, the resulting tiny chemical traces of urea, water and salt drifted away on the gently washing tide. Her cilia felt the chemicals as they pushed by her, and the bitter taste made her wince.

She stared at the coral wall. A deep crack ran through it, and her procreator had worked persistently all her 21 days of life, rasping, pushing his harder shell into the crack, seeking to widen it. Through the wall lay a garden of food, an abundance, lay a glorious profusion of tastes: the tastes of delicacies, of satiation, of repletion.

With a path through the wall, the family could avoid all the dangers (the sharks, the squids, the gaping hungry maws of predators) that circled over the top of their coral bed. The family longed, ached to widen the crack that led straight into the coveted valley—to discover the source of the tastes that so often wafted through the cracks, teetered on the tips of cilia even while sleeping, so that the family would wake, sensing a meal nearby, only to discover merely their coral-walled cave.

Procreator had tried hard with his toughened shell, had tried hard today too, and had stormed out, leaving acrid frustration molecules which hung in the water even now.

She ran her baby's limb up and down the crack—at certain points she could even reach slightly through. The temptation to poke out her cilia and suck at the small particles of food drifting in from the other place was strong...

So slowly, though with pain, she eased the cilia further in and twisted. A whimmer of sound pushed through her skin as pain shot up the soft baby limb.

But had she felt movement, was there an extra wash of current? A little further, and twist. Further and twist...

She could taste blood in the water.

"Just one more try," ran through her brain. Concentrating on pushing hard, she failed to see the anchor from a fishing boat which arced downward crashing into the coral bed.

Pushing hard, she shot suddenly into the garden. Looking back, she saw a crack running from top to bottom of the coral bed and a slippage at its base, forming a narrow tunnel back to home.

Horrified at how her world had shifted, she shot back through the tunnel and cowered in the corner until the family returned home. Then slowly, as a family, they ventured down the tunnel into (their own very special, they felt) garden of delights.

When she later persisted in telling the family how she had forced the crack open, father looked stern, mother scolded, and she wasn't invited to entirely too many parties by neighbours who considered her to be a compulsive liar.

Moral: Even the impossible should be attempted–once.

Chapter 38
STORY: THE SEVENTH

All around was manna–elixir for the body, endorphins for the brain. He tunneled, he twisted, he chewed the soft, soft pliability of muscles decayed, of vole once living now made succulent.

"All because I dared go up near the Blue Abyss!" he exulted. "All because I avoid the Great Wall down low." He paused at a particularly good bit which melted in his mouth without needing his 53 teeth, exulting in his discovery.

A trace of adamantine ran just a half twist away–an all-day cruncher there. He could almost hear his queen urge him to the nutritious vein–but this other: it was new, it tingled and fizzled away in his mouth, and it was ... new!

Newness!–he craved it.

Adamantine was rumoured to be the very core of the earth, down, down below the Indivisible Wall. It was life, it was the best of diets, it was quality vintage. But newness lurked upward–the nearer the Blue Abyss, the more life scintillated, the more life wriggled, throbbed and grew. He had had his moments though, he thought, as he plunged through round whiteness into soft jelly. Yesterday, he had found a long round tunnel full of breathing. Nevertheless he had launched into it, nibbling his way up the wall when there had been a soft rush of iron from out of the velvet darkness–it had only been a stone outcrop that had saved him, although the wetness that had gurgled from a nether wound alternately stung and numbed him even now.

When he had reported it to the Queen and Council last night, all she had snarled was, "Grow up!"–someone had even snickered about up-side-up thinkers–a reference to a common infantile behaviour aberration of persistence in moving with their eyes upward toward the Blue Abyss rather than downwards towards the Wall. He acknowledged that he himself had had the problem for a while before it had corrected itself–but he'd be dashed if he could see what it had to do with the current situation. He had prayed to the great supreme spirit, had gone exploring, and it had ended in disaster. But why should that mean he shouldn't keep trying!

Although there had been that time five sleep-cycles ago when he had prayed, moved into the Uppers, and had heard a rumble like a thinker near him. It had persisted and persisted, so it couldn't have been a fletch passing. Finally he just had to know, and started to nibble away the intervening layers of soft Mother's Kiss rock. Downward and to the left. Downward and to the left.

Wetness on his face and front stopped him. Fear soared. Water—the dread enemy. Somehow he turned and scrambled up the (by new) muddy embankment, only to slide down so his netherness was wedged in the hole.

Dazed, he sagged for some seconds. When he recovered, the water had risen no higher. As he started to move forward, he felt water rush past his netherness—so, at a loss, he sat his netherness down tightly and thought. At length there was only one conclusion. So he twisted his head, chewed the wall and extruded it from his nether regions. Repeat upon repeat upon repeat, hoping that the goo produced would harden.

Finally he was able to make his escape and return to the colony—but he did not share the details of his adventure that night.

It wouldn't have mattered. He could have recited their responses. A tart "Grow up!"" or worse, from the Queen, snickers from her retinue, and perhaps even a recitation from creedlore chanted with all the fervours and desires and longings of a thousand hearts:

Down in the ground, the sound grows faint
Of fletch, or vole, of schwabbly-waint.
Down in the ground the glory soars,
Until you reach th' Indivisible Wall!

Venturing out the next day, up, up into the Adventure, he found a stash of vole left from 3 sleep-cycles ago. As his teeth sliced through a particularly succulent bone down into the rich redness of the centre, he idly tried to make a counter-rhyme:

Up, up up there to sup,
but somehow got stuck on the next line
On things as rare as . . .um

"Melt in your mouth microbites" didn't seem quite right. Nor "adamantine rings..." Mmm.

Well, he decided, time for home anyway. Rippling a heavy stomach over troublesome sharp rocks, he uttered a brief prayer to the supreme spirit to speed his exploration into the unknown. He crested a sharp up-jutting rock and over....

Down, down he tumbled, a steep ravine ripping at his being. Gasping, tumbling, he found the bottom.

He lay there, trying to recover. But a question gnawed—just after prayer, this? What did it mean? Were there things appointed whilst other things were variable?

No, no, a right to explore. Anger gave adrenalin aid–and up and up! He would explore. Up, up, and the ground warmer. Up, up and there seemed a kiss of blueness to the soil which seemed illuminated now. Up, up, and a sound of movement, almost of song.

Two larger hardnesses plunged into the soil and lifted him between two yellow elongations up, up, into the nothingness of air under a Blue Abyss. He looked down into the eyes and body of a schwabbly-waint. Its feathers mirrored those described in the myths.

The bird gulped, and the creature with the strange markings was gone. Frustrated, the bird sighed. There must be something more to life than digging for earth-eaters, even if this one was especially pretty.

Nearby a seed pod on a tree gathered feathers in the sunlight.

Moral: There's a time to go, and a time to stay.

Chapter 39
STICK GROPES THE MEASURE

"Beachhead attempted; failed". He hurled away the report. That his resume would hold this summary was galling; for it to be reported about a Operational Strategy Grade E- was stupefying, bewildering; it mirrored the classic biped who destroys independent mobilization ability by tripping whilst walking on tiny slippery fauna, like the fashion-conscious female who realises she has gone half the day with the back of her dress tangled up in her belt. Creatures such as on this planet were prone each and every day to such inglorious failings as these, and yet he, he, he, had been bested whilst storming such a "gift of a planet"–it was enough to staunch all pride he had ever felt in any work done anywhere in any time era. Even the high risk operations would bleach away under such blistering heat of ridicule as this would raise.

It was the Doctor triumvirate, of course, that had caused the watershed. Like a lost chess game that could have been won in two moves, like a sacking for incompetence one day short of long service leave, he felt the whining flood of impotence.

It had seemed automatic, easily guided, smoothly done:- to, by magic (real magic), lead the inhabitants astray; beginning in one small park often frequented by the Doctor, to lead such a revolution of multiplying pathways so as to obscure, obfuscate and plausibly deny the possibility of any useful and meaningful truth. Once on the deviating path, each inhabitant could be allowed to engage in fruitless (though faultless) activity– to lie in their own urine; to see a sign like a spiderweb as a sign of divine protection; even, glories of glories, to string up, truss up one of the Others. When the son had taken the form of an planet inhabitant and he, he, Stick, had wired him to death, he thought a king hit made.

Failed...

...like the washing, the fading, of a footprint in the sand by a successfully incoming tide...

And now he had been informed that the two were bidding farewell, were promising more aid by leaving them alone (whatever that meant). As if the inhabitants skimming a black hole's event horizon alone without aid suddenly were endowed with greater aid.

But times, indeed Stick's times here had been flavoured with pleasantries, with all the discord of a job well done. The losing of reality by an inhabitant when a lie they heard about a lie formed a epileptic cycle of falsehood so that believing either or both lies placed them beyond understanding the truth, and to link one lie to reason and the other to overwhelming positive emotion, so they seesawed between the extremes. The selective and repeated revealing of hurtful truth to those it would hurt most whilst pinning them beyond any hope of removing themselves from the focused flame...

But this planet was the first blot on his resume—and that of his two friends. So many worlds of rabid success: worlds whose consistent greatest achievement was in progressively finding more and more efficient ways of killing each other. Worlds where each being was lost in a multitude of deceits held up by each inhabitant against the other, none daring reveal their inner being, inner feelings, inner doubts and questions. Worlds where only the killing leads to the living. Worlds so askew they only needed a small touch, a small spin every now and then—they could be trusted to wing their own blazing descent of destruction into a cliff that they themselves had just built.

And now this missive from HQ:- "Assessment: Beachhead attempted; failed."

Suddenly he drove his knife through it, but it simply reformed, untouched. By sitting there, it implicitly called for and then gave verdict on their performance..

And it went further—it recalled them, all of them, the three. It recalled them in shame, in inglory. It recalled them to questionable futures, to possible tortures.

And it went further—as the three receded, it called for the Snake Corp to "favourably terminate the current debacle". Stick reshaped his physical form outline that had just briefly loosened its tightness (in the closest estimate his species had to what this planet's inhabitants would call a shudder).

If they were coming, it was time to go.

Yes, the three were going home, clearing flesh forms appropriate to this planet, climbing execution hill, chasing the setting sun, fading off this stick of planetary rock.

Tonight!

Chapter 40
TAHLA EXPOUNDS II

The Doctor's a shoving leopard,
I nab everything I heed.
He lafes me and mine born in green pastures.
He see-saws my roll.
He guides in polite wrath for His Name's sake.
Although I dork in the valley of shadow of wet,
I will not fear, for mocha is with Dee.
Your shepherd shod, and your raft towel and pect me.
You beeper a pancake for me
And welcome me as an honoured gent.
Morley shot geese, and Nurseries shall
follow me down the lanes in my life.
I'll die in the health of my soul.
Health forever! Amen.

Translation in Appendix.

Chapter 41
A BETTER GOODBYE

Lunch–what could be better?

We three sat chewing and leaning against the wall. A voice floated to us. "Trees lose their leaves–they come back in the new season. People do leave; but in this case, the one leaving will return."

The son! The son was walking down the road behind us. Although the brick wall was between us, I knew his voice.

"Somewhere there's a place as much part of me as the smell of freshly mown grass is for you. Like a spring tautened, cut suddenly, I leave; like the first offer of shade after years in the desert sun, I move with focus; and like the yielding of the last string on a beautifully wrapped present to reveal the treasure inside, I give way to another.

"I know that melancholy uncoils itself as a snake from the corners of your mind and squeezes your hearts with its dread embrace. But I will return–the gladdest summer day holds a sense of my return; the reaching of two hands, lover towards lover, a dim idea of how I long to return. Together we will savour the sweetness after swallowing the bitterness; together we will rest after a sleepless night...

"But for now, I leave."

And my world died, its fabric unravelling at the touch of sound. I stared a stranger in the face of a favoured friend. I groped the burning shipwreck of hopes somewhere on an alien shore. The flaying of some soul I realised was mine. The falling of a flaming sun, racing below the horizon...

...when could the sun, when would the sun rise?

A lonely time was coming. We gawped at each other, we three. At each other like strangers together under a reality too big to hold or understand.

A melted eternity later, the son and his followers came into sight as the brick wall ended, and crossed the road into the park near the school, where he stopped. People seemed to come from everywhere, gathering to him.

And us three up, poured across school fences, tumbled down like waterfalls on the other side, joined the flood, rushed as torrents into the lake around him, and we came to tumbled swirled stillness.

On the edge of the crowd a familiar school teacher. But nothing mattered—only the moment. Only his words... We all listened, like ears with numbness inside.

"I want you to go and tell all you can about me. Invite them to follow me, to take my hand once in love and be changed. And then to take my hand day by day and learn of me. Tell them not to be ashamed of the public declaration of their faith in me. Where you are, into whatever situation you sail, I am there, your captain, your sailing companion, your friend—always."

Then he smiled. "Let me add something—or someone—to you." He glowed, and a thousand white fragments rose from his transfigured self, rose into the air, and drifted in some caressing way into each beating chest, just above our hearts.

"Now I am with you always. Speak to one another of me. The Aider—he whom you have received—will remind you, recall to your mind, all I and my father have told you. And he will take of mine and teach it to you, through many voices, many years, many ways." And he gave Tahla who had moved his way somehow and stood beside him, a small squeeze around the shoulder, and I was sure I felt a white glow from where the Aider had nestled, somewhere close the heart.

"He will comfort, will train, will sustain, will lead. Comfort one another with these words, in adversity and attrition, in sleekness of soul and starvation of body, in the triumph of the minute and the slow grinding of the years. I am there, I am here." And again a warm echo of the Aider in my breast.

"From now one, all those who learn of me, who begin to hold me dear, who cling in devotion to the Name, will have Aider given upon belief, not as you. Blessed are you who see me and believed. Blessed more are they who hear you and believe, for their faith is perhaps a littler taller.

"Speak to one another in psalms and hymns and spiritual songs. Do not forsake the assembling of yourself together, and all the more as you see the End Day approaching. I will never ever leave you–no! nor ever forsake you. With the love you have seen in me, love each other sincerely from the heart. Do all things without grumbling, with melody in your heart to the Doctor.

"Wash each one their own soul, by confessing sins and receiving forgiveness from the Doctor. And forgive others for the ways they let you down–or worse. Love each of you his neighbour. Be forethinking as foxes, and as gentle as doves.

"Pray always in all circumstances, with all vigilance and purity. There is a friend who is closer you than a brother." And the Aider glowed in response.

"The Day will come when I toss the sky aside as a blanket, and come. Comfort one another."

And suddenly he vanished, but the Aider and adrenalin surged like anaesthetic, and somehow I was OK.

But still–I gawked left, right, up. Where was he?

Giants suddenly dotted themselves among the large crowd, close enough to each of us so all could hear. "Why are you standing there, looking up at the sky?" they rumbled. "This son, who was taken from you into heaven, shall return in the sky as royalty, as a bridegroom coming for his bride."

And each giant became a tiny pinpoint of light. The lights coalesced, then sped into the sky so quick.

We looked at each other in Aider's comfort. On the edge of the crowd a school teacher left quickly.

Slowly we all began to move away, each to a house, a workplace, a classroom. I found Tahla and Alla-wuz and we slowly picked our way amongst the groups–back towards the school.

Someone in front of us slumped to the ground, groaning, "All those years wasted . . . useless . . ." But Tahla put his hand on his shoulder.

"Believe in the Doctor, believe in the Son .

He goes to prepare a place for us,

And if he goes to prepare a place for us,

He will take us. That where he is, there we may stay as well.

Blessed dimension, blessed place."

He seemed better. "Thank you," he said, with a grateful look into Tahla's eyes. And he up and moved away.

Chapter 42
BIRD AS HAWK

Stretching . . . and caught! Getting two fingers on the fire escape door as it started to swing shut, Mrs Falpub slipped into the stairwell. With a quite silent "thank you", she slipped up the stairs and out onto her floor. The door clicked hollowly shut, and she into her room and to the teacher's desk.

She found the desk key, and scrabbled frantically for the orange and red striped book. She flicked it open randomly and thumbed through. Good, the names of the students had been written in already, one per page as required. At least bureaucracy had saved her that much time.

A sudden suspicion struck her and she quickly flicked to the front of the book—was it the current year? Mmmm, there it was—all in order. The year was neatly written under the usual heading:

Register of Student's Engagement
in Subversive Activities
*(to be kept by one person
for entire school year)*

Oh how she hated this part of the job, she thought wearily to herself. Just finished seven years watching her next-door neighbour's kid all through school—and now here was the next intake—joined by the eyeball for seven years.

And nothing she could do. Her mother's drugs cost too much. The money must keep flowing, or her mother would. That wretched urine disease that struck last year had laid mother low, had wasted her so quickly, wasted her until a loving daughter had accessed restricted drugs, only available to Government workers such as she. But the price had been dear—she felt like a stake marked Government Property had been embedded in her soul. And ropes and tension stretched from the stake into all corners of her life—her self-respect, her ethics, her time...

...and her love—there had been a man, a man in whose arms you could hide as within the comfort of walls—in the comfort of love, of solace, of warmth. There had been...

It's only been a year, she thought... The pain must end soon...

But she put down her pen and looked out the window, looked at the clouds drifting through their lives. Little buttons of softness, amidst some larger clouds building.

Even they seemed to brood above her, so she sighed and turned back to the book, opening at the first student's entry.

She read the name "Umenies, Sulk", sighed in relief–no problem there. And for the next, and the next. Good! Turning the page, she found the name "Mej, Tahla", and she sat back suddenly. The Doctor and his son were on the subversive's list, and Tahla–well after this morning–there was just no question.

So she leant to write: "Strong links with Doctor's son. Must..."

She brushed away a tear angrily. How could a five year old child (no relation) remind her so much of her ex?

There had been good times: the letters; the kisses. And she slipped into her favourite daydream: standing at the window, her hand resting on his letter she had just read and her head in the thousandth heaven with him, when a squeak of the gate causes her to look down, and there he is, the hand on the gate post, looking up with that "I'll take on the world and love it" grin. And...

Yes, there had been the good times.

And they two lurking, mere months ago, at the edge of crowds gathered around the doctor; listening while pretending to admire the mountain in the distance, the display in the shop window, the flowers in the garden across the road. Listened while half-discussing people they knew, places, times, things–anything to linger longer without the Government realising why there were really there. They both knew the black-humoured adage

Is the bug bugged?

Is the sky too high?

They even had a code when they wanted to discuss the Doctor's words, his movements, his sayings. "Aunt Maude this..." and "Aunt Maude did that...", and so they could talk just a little of the Doctor 'neath the listening skies. But then her mother had fallen ill, and Aunt Maude and Mum in public view was just too big a price. Then the risk, then the government doctors, then the sustaining, then the limbo... then this current status in between life and existence...

It was then that that she had lost her man, too. Just as she had pulled back from her fledging trust, he had gone overt:- the public stand, the private goodbye, the travelling and the telling and the witnessing.

And her losings...

She still believed, still held Aunt Maude dear, although she had cost her. Still held the son high in her heart, and today's giving had not been a stranger to her. That the son was with her in a deep and deep way, she knew.

As she had leaned to write, "Strong links with Doctor's son. Must...", there had been a sadness, almost a sense of grieving, near her heart.

She looked out the window. The clouds had thickened slightly, hiding the sun, and she longed somehow to reach up, just brush the clouds aside, let the warmth through. But it was impossible, and that was that. She learnt again. If she didn't report the children, someone else would, and she would be found out, and mother would be turned out, the tablets stopped, and a wasting, and a fading, and the fading...

"Too much, too much," she muttered. "To work, to work."

And outside, metal fingers raced above the sky; below, there were the shrieks of children at play.

Chapter 43
TAHLA EXPOUNDS III

"Mow!" I tell Lou. "Wisterias we will slot all neat," but
she, well, bally changed in a moment, in the twinkling of
an eye–fat!! The past lump, it... I mean, at the last
trumpet. For the trumpet shall round, sound, and
the dead Shelly braised. (Hun's itchy!) Bull, the vet is
dolled up. Swim, hickory!!
The death is swallowed up in victory.

Translation in Appendix.

Chapter 44
SNAPPETS

exhaust
time exhaust
old time exhausted
the old time is exhausted

trains
change trains
change trains speed
change, like trains, comes at different speeds

sweat
even sweat
even hot sweat
even hot sweat changes
even hot sweat brings beneficial changes

cascades
cascades my
cascades my brow
cascades love my brow
changes cascades, as love, across my brow

Chapter 45
STORY: THE EIGHTH

Ronald Mouse had a problem. He was as cross-eyed as the worst cross-eyed fly you'd ever see. And we've all seen cross-eyed flies, the way they try to fly straight in the air and never can quite manage it. They weave, they twist, and get just so scared whenever someone moves towards them. Well, Ronald Mouse was all these things and more.

The elderly professor, who kept him as a pet and loved him very much, was proud of how Ronald had coped with life in his large multi-floor cage. All by himself, Ronald had invented the "Blink, blink, think" routine: close the left eye, look with the right; then close the right eye, look with the left; open both eyes, think really hard, then move. It was always in the right direction, and the kind professor had become very proud.

After a while, sadly, Ronald grew tired of such hard thinking, so much so that the professor wondered what had come over him. Ronald grew fond of rituals to get him through his home. Main hallway was three hops with the left side, three hops with the right, then half a double hop to the hole down to the next floor. After a while it became clear that two spins just before starting was enough to keep the hops just the right distance, so he finished in just the right place—after two weeks of the spin and hops, he just knew there was no other way.

Second floor was even trickier. There was a reflection of himself about halfway along, just before the bend, and it always terrified him—the great fat black shape wobbling towards him as he moved gracefully toward it. and so he found that a fast sprint towards the strange shape, hit the wall on the left, and bounce to the right, worked very nicely.

On ground floor, there was the three-spin difficulty, on second floor the T-turn, and on the top floor there was the "back your way along the precipice, both eyes closed" (no one should have to endure what that looked like cross-eyed), and there was the walk on two legs like a confused beetle at that awkward spot near the food tray.

All things that had worked once, and so Ronald kept them instead of thinking...

It was pretty clear that "Blink, blink, think" had gone, and the professor worried and fretted. Finally he took Ronald out of his glass-edged box and totally remodeled it—three food trays, each with two of Ronald's absolute favourite treats, scent trails to lead him to them, new twists and turns to bring back "Blink, blink, think", and bright clear lights everywhere so that "Blink, blink, think" would be easy.

So Ronald was put back into his home, full of new pleasures, built with love.

But Ronald Mouse hated it. He tried to charge down the main hallway but got a very bruised nose AND the hallways were too narrow for spinning AND on the third floor there was no dangerous edge to back along whilst feeling terrified.

So he sulked, found the deepest, darkest, quietest part of his home and lay there for days, moodily chewing the floor. The professor, seeing all this, coaxed him, studied him lovingly, rewarded even the tiniest move back to "Blink, blink, think", but Ronald Mouse, although he slowly got fat, never got the point.

One day, the Professor thought, "Just one more day to make a breakthrough. Otherwise I'll take him to a circus or TV show where strange behaviour is definitely loved."

And he sighed.

Moral: If you don't accept necessary change, you may still be useful in a minimalist comic way

Chapter 46
THOUGHT

Hand in hand
        with a bigger hand,
A child accepts change,
        seeing only the hand.

Chapter 47
TAHLA EXPOUNDS IV

Without graindoor, puddy, this starry mocha is studenders–
He who was flown in showerish;
Proven by the aider;
Seen by the unseen world;
Discussed oft with neighbours;
Accepted with love by the world;
Now risen to his glory.
                    Translation in Appendix.

Chapter 48
TAHLA EXPOUNDS V

The Doctor is our rest-hinge and strong hold
A traymaids any time.
I will not shear foes, though the world should change,
Though the mountains should shake in the heart of the sea,
Though its waters grow fur and roam.
Even if a fellow worker understands change better than me
And is promoted while I demote,
Even if a chosen career is irrelevant after a change...
Even if at the end of life, there is nothing to show but that
I did fruitfully in an outdated job.
I smell Shilo!
For the Doctor is a shoving leopard.   *Translation in Appendix.*

Chapter 49
THE CALL

I'll push the bounds to stir you on,
Grip hot coals to urge you find
A Doctor's love for you.
I'll bend walls out to aid you on,
Grip the nettle to let you see
The supply of what a life
does need.
I'll take clenched fists. Still do what's right,
Pull limbs apart, but still know that light
Can, will, and still does, wait right now for you.

Chapter 50
SITUATION OF INTEREST

"Travel Pod 115316 landed. 115316." He tiredly flipped off the recorder and stretched. 7000 years of arthritis bubbled and snapped in his backbone. He smiled wanly–once the blood lust hit, he would be OK, the body would work, would writhe, would move as well as ever. Eye slits contracted at the thought, tail twitched.

"Commence disembarkation procedures," echoed over the ship's speaker system, and willingly enough, he uncoiled himself from the control stick, and arose. Tucking his tail tip carefully between his two fangs, and flexing so as to form a wheel, as was the custom of his battalion, he rolled out the cockpit and down the long, now empty, aisles, and into the thundering fever of the hunt.

He rolled almost carelessly down the ramp and out onto grass. He glanced up at the sky. Blue tint, with one white sun of the type that inhabitants of such worlds wearily persisted in labelling "yellow", although no one really knew why.

No need to wait! Information about missions and objectives flooded into his neural link:-

Subvert knowledge or subtract life from sympathizers of Others' beachhead, given probable imminent evacuation of Others from said beachhead.

Minimal possibility of entering new phase of Others' operations.

List of targets for this terminal...

Thereupon followed list after list of names. He grunted–"beachhead" had been too gentle a word–this had been a very successful Others' foray.

There was a lot of work here.

He mentally accessed "Geographic data" and it poured into his mind, took its place in an orderly fashion, synapse by synapse, association by association ; and customs, lifeform characteristics, societal distinctives and lifeform daily sustenance regimes paraded tidily in his distributed neural pathways. He accessed "Most Likely Enemy Position" and watched markers dot up around the display.

He decided to aim for the nearest dense grouping. While powering up, he mentally flipped past the *Wisdom of the Moment* display:

Tell two lies to a lifeform; the best second lie creates a self-sufficient internal lie with the first.

"Fool a lifeform for 2000 heartbeats; they'll see it as a reliable experience for eternity.

"Lifeforms happily eat froth, but grumble at solid food.

"Lifeforms can only discriminate between truth and two false mirrors. Give them three false mirrors and the truth will be rejected too.

"You can give pleasure or pain. Pleasure leads more effectively to the desired goal.

"Confuse and suspend a lifeform between two alternatives. Throttling them then feels twice as sweet.

"Their tech makes them free, their magic makes us free.

"Even the most minor foothold allows us to take another step.

"Their blood or yours–it makes no difference to HQ.

"To even contemplate giving less than your best is punishable by one hour torture by the Black Guards.

"By Order HQ"

He mentally flipped (more slowly) past the visual recordings of "Highlights of the Last Campaign" with pride–one key preliminary moment in there had been his (before the last failed contingent had arrived). Behind him, the ship winked out, and he too switched on the Phase Slip and commenced deployment.

He rolled sight unseen, senses untouched, through the nearest rural dwelling … and through the baby just inside.

On a whim, he rolled back into her, found her terror setting, and jammed it to max for 20 seconds. The screams brought in a larger…–was it?–yes, a female, scurrying from the next room.

Chuckling, he moved on. Then impatiently, he slammed "Resilience" to high, and bounced.

Up and forward, up and forward, clearing the houses, the trees, then the nearest cliff. He exhilarated and idly aimed at another lifeform. Slamming down from a two kilometre height, rippling through their body, then up, up, while the lifeform walked on oblivious.

Time to try out his reflexes. He slammed down and through and up in a driver of a– access memory, yes–car, opaquing just at the eye level. He looked back as he soared–yes, the driver, blinded, had swerved into the path of an oncoming semitrailer, and was a fraction of his former self.

Something more demanding? So he found a cyclist, and as he slammed through him, imprinted the magnified image of an oncoming car onto his brain. The thirteen year old suddenly saw what was a distant car suddenly apparently immediately in front of him, and slammed on the brakes. As the initiator soared, he saw the car behind hit at speed.

Ah, red blood, just as the neural upload had said.

Another test–data retrieval and imprint. Spying a communal children's gathering place, he decided to slam through, retrieve the maternal face image and imprint it on the large ball being passed back and forward between three beings. Ignoring the floppy-eared one, he poured himself down the tunneled trajectory into, through, his target.

He hit, soared. Soared high–too high…

He hovered, hit "Incident Review" playback, set to max slow.

…

He had not penetrated.

The being had not been penetrated!

Diagnostics!!

No faults. He slammed four other children and an adult cozener in the region, imprinting on each a brief nightmarish flash. Procedures were fine.

Slam the failed target. Down, down, down…

Failure.

Approach the target! Observation! Whirling around its head, multiple viewing modes…

Nothing. A static blip near its heart, which stubbornly refused to go away. The two closeby targets showed evidence of the same…

Growl into its ear. Good–no problems.

Penetrate … now!

Failure.

Still, there seemed a possible opening. But he saw at once it needed to be opened from the being's internal region.

Puzzled he S'ed himself over a nearby power pole. Communicatives from other field operatives were reporting much the same through secure communications.

Adder Company had arrived, and they had found a situation of interest. The Others once again had proved quite creative.

Chapter 51
STORY: THE NINTH

"And now the cat!" and they sprang forward, each striving to project the most convincing, yet humorous, cat. One camera man trying to get too close, was driven back by an indignant, spitting clawed beast; while other cameras pivoted, rushed, recorded the images for the TV audience. Another pleaded with the camera for food, developed a double-jointed back, so he weaved teasingly through the cameraman's legs—in struggling to maintain the image, the cameraman stumbled, falling against the extra-large stage-prop bowl of milk-simulant placed on stage, capsizing it.

The stage director chuckled. This could well be the best show ever. "And now—dog ... sounds!" came the request, and the four creatures launched into their carefully researched act. The audience loved it. The four creatures, each a different species, were such gifted character actors that the audience could not help but be persuaded each time by the new portrayals.

It had been an excellent 60 years, thought the director, rubbing his whitening fur. The four actors had started much the same time as he, and together they had ridden a golden highway—and there was no reason why it should ever stop. Listen to that audience!!

And the ratings were consistently high.

And there would soon be a special twist this very episode—not even the actors knew what it would be. Only on such a show with such caliber as this one would one ever dare to do that! These actors had seen it all, had done it all, were ready...

Loud guffaws shook the audience's sides, and pulled him out of his reverie. Well, that was one he'd have to see tonight on the re-runs.

"And change ... cockroach. Cryptic fragmented." And they moved smoothly into the most abstract routine, the feathered creature, the furry creature, the reptilian and the human. They held the audience, even in the abstract pieces: as always, he thought—it showed them for the faultless craftsmen they were.

"And change... beetle. Team mosaic."

The upcoming surprise event was the last event. Four minutes had been reserved, and off to one side, stagehands were quietly setting up five chairs in a semicircle facing the audience.

The setup finished, the workers retreated into the darkness, as the mosaic finished. The emcee smoothly guided the creatures, loping or shuffling (according to their individual physiology) to the seats.

"And now, a special treat! A new event!" said the emcee as its head filled the television screens of ten million homes. "Our cast has no idea what will happen next; you have no idea

what will happen next, but," and he smiled a beautiful smile, "I have, and..." He moved back to fill the middle chair in the semi-circle "...it's something you've always wanted!" And again the beautiful smile. "For all fans out there, I present... Be Yourself". Yes, an old-fashioned interview where you can finally find out a little about your favourite stars."

And he turned to the furred star. "What's the most humorous event from your childhood?"

But ... silence.

A beautiful smile, three rapid blinks of an eyelid. Turning to the feathered member, "What was your first crush, your first infatuation, like?"

Feathers rustled, but ... silence.

Another question quickly. Fill the void.

...nothing. Another, and another and another...

...nil.

And he realized, along with the accompanying feeling that he was dying a stage death, that there was no personal remnant left to the four. They had been actors, were actors, had no part inside them that was not dedicated to "The Act".

The emcee suddenly that there would be no answers, were no answers ... and so there could be no questions.

The stage director hurriedly cut to ads—and they were watched by ten billion homes in puzzlement.

Moral: In the midst of change, your core, your self, must remain.

Chapter 52
TAHLA EXPOUNDS VI

For he is the vid-ding loctor,
enduring forever.
He's dinkum, shall never be destroyed.
His pool will never be shut array
Deliveries and vases are made, he
who saved Daniel from harm, from
the lower of the big pylons.

Translation in Appendix.

Chapter 53
STEPPING UP

Changing one trapeze for another
is better when you have a
safety net, have a supervisor
who has proven themselves with
change, and when change
occasionally gets you
an improved cushy job
with your own chair.

Chapter 54
BALLS THAT BOUNCE

The weirdest thing! Tahla was getting ready to catch the ball when a sphere bounced off his head and soared way up high. Unphased, he just caught the rubber ball and threw it back...

Lunch was just so much better than at home. Mum makes me sit after I eat–she really has no idea; how could I rest when sunbaking yonder were the swings, the monkey bars, and even, even the sidesaw!

Mum had never let me on the sidesaw, and here it was, inviting me, welcoming me, and so, so promising... Lunch hour promised so much! Me and Alla-wuz and Tahla: weird kid, but I liked him. We had clicked, just like Alla-wuz and me.

But he was weird! No one else I knew ever had spheres bouncing off their head. Stra-ange!

I saw Mrs Falpub staring out of our classroom window–then saw the ball coming at me out of the corner of my eye. I caught it, passed.

Catch and pass.

Catch and pass.

The sphere returned. Drifting down, it floated around Tahla's head...

And I saw–it looked like a jewelled snake–jewels and metal throwing dappled sunlight-reflections on the ground as it moved.

My reality was stretching... I'd never had an imaginary friend before, let alone an imaginary jewelled snake.

Did imaginary friends start like this? Weren't they for lonelier days, for darker days, for darker eyes?

He bounced into Tahla's ear, bounced out. After a frustrated pause and wriggle, it flew to the top of the electricity pole yonder on the street, draping itself over the wires as lazily as a Sunday afternoon sprawl. It touched two wires but didn't go pfft.

So it couldn't be real, could it?

The whiteness near my heart seemed somehow alert.

Enough with the ball! Over to the funtube. Up the rope mast, down it, stand on the platform, jump into the funnel. Slide, slide, slide to the bottom.

And around and up, racing Tahla to the top, this time he was first on the platform, and first to slide. "I just love the ton food," he shrieked in my ear. Alla-wuz just stood at the bottom–his ears wouldn't fit.

Yonder, the petite feminine fluff from our class seemed to point scornfully at us and say something to the group round her. A laugh drifted across the ground.

Let her have her way–this was heaven.

A jewelled snake, similar to the other, bounced its way across the school ground, bounced up high, and joined the other one on the pole.

"Sigh sword, sidesaw!" yelled Tahla. We and Alla-wuz across to it, onto it. Forbidden fruit indeed. Just like a see-saw, but sideways, that's all. Fast through the middle, slowing down to the furtherest point out, weightless and tireless for half a second; then gathering speed, back back into the rush to the other side, again inhaling the weightless timeless promise of summer.

Heaven! Elixir! I'd found me my pleasure zone. A snake ball bounced across the ground. Turned suddenly, came at my head fast, aiming at my eyes.

Then bouncing away. I had felt nothing! Inside, the Aider passed comfort and strength to fight the adrenalin surge.

Floating back, it hovered near my head. Glowing, jewels above each vertebrae, ruthlessness and craziness around it like a bad smell. Hovered near me. Changed colours: red, purple, silvery like bad mirrors.

I reached up my hand to touch it.

It moved. Suddenly at the other end of the schoolyard. Then back again.

Just out of arm's reach, it bounced to the left. My eyes followed it, watching.

Bounced to the right. Tracking...

Large bounces, and my head moved up and down, like watching a Grand Final Ball game.

Touched Tahla. "Look!"

He played along. "Big wriggly hippos! I used to have imaginary friends too."

"What?"

"Big wriggly hippos. I know. I used to pretend to see them too. Mared my scum, though.'

"No, but..." I tracked the snake with my pointing finger.

Tahla smiled too politely, then turned away.

The second snake, more like a oranger circle, zoomed down from its telephone pole and escorted the other one away at speed. Together, like friends, they disappeared behind the bus stop building.

Chapter 55
WRITING HOME

Top priority to Shipcommand. Pilot 226Y ID Password aMddY. Various inhabitants infiltrated have impermeability factor 7, also sight & tracking factor 7. Both occur even at maxtech modes. Infiltrates' fear/Adrenalin response unusual. Only those infiltrated by Others suspected affected. Pls advise.

Chapter 56
TAHLA EXPOUNDS VII

I know that you dan koo all things, and that no purpose
of yours dan be bopped. You, Stewart, are talking, you to
Will, in the army of the heaven and the inhabitants of the
earth. No one can restrain your hand. You, who sit in the
leavened half, have kibble rings and rulers in derision.
Whenever stinks guide, 'mmediately de-stride to change
your change, yourself. Dang and leaks can come about,
are deposed of, new ones are set up. And set, the very
same ones come humbly, ninging
good brews in your street and in your towns.
Yes, the Doctor cleans up the earth.

Translation in Appendix.

Chapter 57
KEEP YOUR GUARD

I gawped after the fleeing snakes. Hit in the side of the head, I went sprawling.

I looked around frantically to find Alla-wuz and Tahla in hysterics. Near them, the ball we'd been playing with bounced away.

"That was so funny, Amah. Sorry," apologised Alla-wuz, in between gasps for air. "You were so dopey. Just looking into the air like that–we'd been playing ball 'gain for about three minutes, so I just had to pass it to you. So dopey, just so dopey."

"Yeah, ran into any bugles lately…" laughed Tahla.

And they both collapsed into laughter again. Strangely, the group of girls nearby looked slightly sickened.

I laughed and jumped on top of Alla-wuz. A few friendly play-punches, and all was right again.

Then the bell rang the end of lunch, and we paraded back into school. Little Miss Petite sniffed, "Barbarians" as she walked past us to her seat. Perfume swirled in her wake, telling of different worlds, different values.

Mrs Falpub put an orange and black book back in her desk, locked it, then enthralled me–a plant's roots, she said, are like drinking straws for a plant to suck up water and food from the ground–now I know why Mum said my soggy mud pie was only useful to plant something in.

Once again, she's smarter than I thought…

Then craft! And the last hour flew by.

School out, Alla-wuz and I said goodbye to Tahla, who saw his Dad waiting for him, and we started the short walk home.

So we strolled along the street, two best buds, schools kids soon finishing up their first year, reminiscing about the year, about the Doctor, about Stick, Slime and Stretch's attempts to kill him, the attempt to kill the son, our kidnapping, the final victory. And now the son had gone, and the Aider had come. We could guess a little of the Aider's work, but so much we knew we would never know–in that way, he was just like the Doctor, just like the son.

We said goodbye at my gate, and I walked up my footpath, reflecting that change was work…

…but that I was handling it well.

SECTION 3

FIRE NIGHT

Please note: this book is written in a very unusual style. It's really helpful to read the chapter titles. They may be your only clue as to who the chapter is about or to the location of the chapters actions.

There is an explanatory key to Tahla's speech in Appendix A of this book.

Chapter 58
LURKING DEAN

Dawn chinked crystal against my window.

Reluctantly unfurling herself from the house, unfurling from peering in its windows, night looked briefly under trees and in the shadows, then smirking fled frantically down dark gutters and moist holes till the fall of the night.

She would come again...

But I awoke with determination.

All this year, all these holidays there had been calls in the streets at night, calling out a name–"Dean"...

Though the year had just begun and Grade 2 lurked just round the corner, puzzlement propounded. Who was Dean? Why did calls come from the next block even in the afternoon: "Dee-dee-dee-ann," they would call and it would echo back from different vocal cords in the crystal still air of night.

I had a right to know, I declared to the silence in my room. Two years ago, I had been there for the Doctor's defiance of the Three, had watched a son die, then borne by starlight swarms into the Doctor's home. Alive! he was alive! and the world had romped and the stones had sung that night.

And the next year, the start of school, the son leaving and the aider coming, comforting, holding, carrying.

And I had been there—watching, seeing, not understanding it all sometimes . . . but there!

I needed to know. Although there were some eternal mysteries, like why, when I lay, in the backyard with my back against the ground, I always had to grip a little tuft of grass to stop myself falling off this planet...

But I had come to know my world, my neighbourhood. And something was different. Girls with tattoos called dee-dee-dee-ann to wild boys my age, and they smirked silently back. Men in suits whispered it to others and looked a little guilty, like they had strained against respectability and had felt it give a little.

Dean? Who was Dean??

Chapter 59
"WE LISTEN, WE HEAR"

"Hearken, children, and I will tell you the Saga of the Wanderer. And now you're to say 'We listen, we hear."

"Why?"

"Because of the tradition. Tut-tut. The preponderance of accustomed procedure and methodology aids in facilitation of…" and he blinked and calmed. *"Because it's what we do in my culture, children. OK?"*

"OK. We listen, we hear," came from the voices, at perfectly discordant speeds, pitches and volumes.

"Tut-tut. OK…

"One day, a boy got out of—you would call it bed—and the world beckoned."

Chapter 60
TAHLA EXPOUNDS VIII

De-loved, boo! Not be fur-raid of the
tryeree fry-all which is to come.
Stand thinner, Fay!

Translation in Appendix.

Chapter 61
THOUGHT

In the Doctor's relationship to men, just as
in his relationship to his son,

every man is alone
with Him.

Chapter 62
TAHLA EXPOUNDS IX

Kit, you might land! Stree-bong! Rejoice
Always, give thanks in all things.
Hee-haw brays in air for all the saints.

Translation in Appendix.

Chapter 63
TAHLA EXPOUNDS X

So we are always confident,
even though we know that
while we are at home in the body,
we are away from the Doctor—
for we fork by weight,
not by sight.

Translation in Appendix.

Chapter 64
BREAKFAST SONG

I put down my breakfast fork, and asked Dad, "Who's Dean?"

"Dean? Dean who?"

"Everyone is saying it: they go "dee-dee-dee-ann" and giggle and look at each other, and I don't know what it is."

"Just an advertising campaign, I expect."

"Oh... OK."

A pause, while I considered that from all angles... No, it didn't seem to be helping. "What's that?"

"Oh, it's like the orange stuff you're eating there. They sing a little song about it:-

"Offer them the spoon! Mum, use your big spoon!

"Dad, work that big spoon! Kids, grow up big and strong!

"Breakfast is the way to grow! Without it, everything just slows.

"Give me ORNGE, don't give to me fat—

"I'll grow up strong. Now that's a fact."

"It's from the that song I Like Ornge," I said.

"Yes, you like the song, you sing the song, and you want to eat the stuff. People sit down and work hard to write songs, to make you sing the song, to make you want to buy things... That's advertising. Advertising is when you see something on the vids, and want it."

That kinda helped. Then a thought struck me. "Is TV short for The Vids?"

Dad laughed, though I wasn't sure why. "Perhaps it is. Now best get dressed."

And off I scuttled.

Chapter 65
SNAPPET II

Slow
Slow ant
Slow one ant
Slow one, considerant
Slow one, consider the ant's industry

Chapter 66
THOUGHT

How can one be alone? If it were only me and the Doctor versus a protagonist, versus a group, versus an angry mob, it is as if it were me and a power bigger than all the accumulated suns faced perhaps one, or perhaps one hundred, or perhaps one thousand small beings.

We, together, through love and showing love…

Chapter 67
PREPARATION

The shoelaces were stubborn that first morning of school, sliding like wet spaghetti until frustration rose in me and prickled my forehead.

Finally done, I went down to where Mum and Dad were sitting.

Chapter 68
ONWARD LIKE JELLY

He greeted me heartily, then, "Shall we be about our task, my friend?"
I gripped his shoulder with my sinewy bronzed hand that had seen the heat of a thousand battles, and replied in a shaky voice almost firmly under control, "To the fray, my friend."
And we turned and began.

Chapter 69
WHISKERS ARE CLOSE

I turned away from Alla-wuz's house in disgust. What was the use of a best friend when he was sick on the first day back at school...

Moodily, I up the street alone, past Tahla's house which nestled near mine–he was out of town with his dad at the beach and was back tonight–and I started the long walk towards school.

Dogs snuffed and pulled owners up the street, joggers dared their bodies, and calls of "dean" rippled the morning air. The promise of happiness hung just within consciousness, and large stones bit into the soles of my shoes, meeker stones fled my approach.

I traced a long crack in the sidewalk past four houses, until I got too close to a boarded fence, and a dog yammered. I jumped back, sobered...

The day hung on me like a second-hand pair of trousers–baggy in all the wrong places. Without my friends, the road was too long, the sun was too close, and I had oh so much time on my hands.

To occupy nuisance time, I let my mind roam over the last three years. How Alla-wuz and I (best buds forever, Yay!) had seen the magicians come, amaze everyone, and somehow spread a plague across the city like stardirt. And then the Doctor had come–I remembered how that first day he had walked past me and how that, near his feet, each blade of grass had clapped hands with its neighbour–duos of one-armed men clapping his entrance. And around him had swirled a myriad of lights, each one of which could, in an instant, turn into a mighty giant, and then, just as quickly, back into a dancing brilliant adoring pinpoint.

And the magicians had tried to kill him, but he just disappeared, and their knives and blades had descended, slicing empty clothes. Alla-wuz and I had seen the bewilderment in their faces as they picked up empty clothes sliced so finely...

Oh, and there was Tahla, before we became second-best buds forever (Yay!), who at night wandered into one of the magicians and was enveloped in a bubble. And it had contracted and contracted till all his juices ran out and he became just a small black stone, such as in any street gutter. And the son, the son had bought him back to life. And the son, then–was just the same, pulped...

And a thousand weeping pinpoints had borne him along the road to the Doctor's House, and there the Doctor (still alive) re-newed his son's body. And the family was forever together again. But together they left here left this place left this planet; and Aider had come. For each one who trusted the Doctor, Aider now lives inside them, strengthening, helping, sometimes warning.

Like when the bouncy techno-snakes came. Only I was able to see them, and they just bounced through people like they weren't there–ping-pong balls, bouncing around the playground. Aider was troubled in me, and yet I had reached out, had wanted, had almost touched it... I had seen it hunt or terrify two other kids in the playground, and yet I had wanted to...

Alla-wuz and Tahla couldn't see it, wouldn't believe me, thinking I was developing an imaginary friend. I snorted. Imaginary friend, indeed!–invisible barracuda, more-like.

I snapped out of my reverie to find I was standing still and that I was still facing over half of the steep hill. Turning around, I could see my own street and house lay only a short distance away.

Sighing, I turned back to the hill, and counted footsteps as I walked up it. One left, one right, two left, two right, up and up on a baggy day...

I heard the sound of a jogger behind me, and moved to one side. Then I heard a voice. "Want lunch today?" and I turned.

"Mum!"

"You forgot your lunch, Amah, and I thought I'd catch up with you–you hadn't been gone that long. No-one else with you today?"

"No. Alla-wuz was sick... And Tahla is still on holidays."

"Lucky-duck him! Can I walk to school with you today?"

"Oh ... ok." I didn't dare seem too eager, but inside I was dancing. Mum always knew the right thing to do!

So we walked, and the houses flew by, and we talked and she was so interested. Some adults–well ...

We parted at the corner before school, and I ducked in through the side gates. Down past the sports area, down past the swings and ...

I stopped. In the sandpit, all alone was Jort. I shrunk back out of sight. He hadn't seen me since that day just before first grade, when he'd almost killed me. He hadn't seen me today yet either, and if I had my way, he never would ... For a whole year and a bit, I'd dodged and weaved, ducked and dodged.

("More power to the artful dodge!" scurried across a frightened mind.)

He finished in the sandpit and ran down towards the school building, leaving the area deserted. It was my chance! and I quickly up and sprint-walked down past the large swing, past the sandpit...

I stopped. Written in Jort's scrawl were the letters

D D D N

DDDN I repeated to myself, and something connected–it sounded like "Dee-dee-dee-ann," and I stared, mystified.

There was a sound behind me, and I turned to see Jort, close, oh so close, behind me. We stared at each other, recognition naked in both our eyes.

"You! I . . ." he stuttered. And then a sneer. "Ridden any good norses yet? Had any good tumbles yet? Oh . . . seen any good doctors yet? Oh! Loved any good gravestones yet, haha?

"It isn't over," he continued with rising venom. "I still owe you . . .

". . . or maybe you owe me, and I always, always get paid . . . sooner or later."

Suddenly he lunged past me, and smeared out the letters in the sandpit. He smiled arrogantly, diffidently at me.

"It's a secret, you see. . ." he said, and then ran off towards school.

Knees weak, I sat on the sandpit's edge. Fate hovered around my head like hungry sharp teeth, and the day breathed its lost breath with gulps.

I thought of Tahla who often transposed letters of words when he spoke. Of how, on the first day in Grade 1, he had proudly told the teacher. "Nigh maim is Tahla".

I gloomily felt I could identify with the first two words.

"Nigh maim" indeed. . .

Chapter 70
JELLY

It was early, oh so early, and the classroom gaped at Mrs Falpub in black misery–silence poured too easily into the aching void. If only she hadn't had that dream last night–the one where she awoke trembling at the sudden loss of something big, of something life-completing, of something too too near her to be named.

She had stumbled up, and had tried to lose herself in preparing notes for her class–the maths sheets needed improving and she had immersed herself mercilessly in them. Then, tend to Mother when she rose, give her the vital government-supplied drugs only available to approved citizens, and to school. Immerse, soak and drown, immerse, soak, and drown the ache away.

And yet, and yet, half an hour later, she was blubbering like a stunned puppy. She crossed to the window and stared across the road.

There were grey days and black days, and this could well be the blackest yet. He was somewhere in the city, she knew, and was about the Doctor's work–too much in love with Him to care to hide his commitment away, for him to toe the safe Government line. She had had no choice–lose the safety of being a good citizen, and she would lose those precious drugs which kept Mum alive.

But still she remembered the magic of two lips on a summer night, the flower scent heavy in the air. . .

The dream pushed back into her consciousness, bull-dozed happiness. She remembered how in the dream he had knelt, he had covered her with a blanket of perfect warmth. Then he had turned, he had turned to leave with the Doctor, and he caught a blanket thread on his shoe clasp as he turned, as he left. And she had called out but the blanket unravelled, unravelled until the cold poured in.

She had awoken then. But somehow falling asleep again, dreamed and it seemed that he had filled her soul with perfect fluid sweetness, with completion; but he turned to go, he turned to go with the Doctor and he knocked the bath plug holding in all the warmth, the glory—and slowly it drained to emptiness. And again he came and filled her lungs with dancing vitality, with dances, until turning to leave, he left the air that she needed suddenly deadened, thickening, turning to jelly.

Breathing, then not breathing ... then not breathing ... then gasping, she awoke in cold sweat to a room empty, a room of dead air, a room of coldness, a room of choking uselessness and trembling.

He had heard the Doctor's call, and she could not follow and her love had kissed her, kissed as he left.

She had felt heaviness then, but this growing emptiness filled her soul and more—a soul tasting little warmth, only feeling duty and tending others, but never, never herself.

Chapter 71
JOURNAL OF P ULYSSES PLUGRATH III– ENTRY 125

When they come like a rolling storm front, I must be with them, or the lightning strikes. When they thunder down streets, I must thunder with them, or I become a tumbleweed—and who knows how long before I stop tumbling.

They are many, and they know me. They know that I know their plans—they shared them with me, and the trap was sprung. Now I am with them, or I am dead.

A poet, a man with a musical soul, I am in troubled times. Still, although many may die, I must survive. My duty is to set down such things as disturb my soul, to hold a mirror to our troubled times, to allow society to see its soul, and to have it blink at itself in disgust.

I am in this thing, but value lies in the recording of it! Perhaps...

When the trouble dragon snorts
and raises its hot hot head,
I look away to a time

when trouble lies dead,
and care is a snore,
and nameless beauty has come in my sight,
but I dare not look–
or I am undone.

Yes, perhaps a quest for nameless beauty in the midst of ugliness and death is my calling, is my placement by fate at this time.

They are so many–what can I do?

Chapter 72
JOURNAL OF P ULYSSES PLUGRATH III– ENTRY 125 POSTSCRIPT

We await the signal DDDN.

Strange–it sounds almost musical, a line from a chorus in a play. But plays can be comedies or tragedies...

Quick notes for possible poem:-

> Well-to-do gentleman in a restaurant–nursing mother and her infant.

> Both content and confident in their worlds.

>But when disaster strikes, what counts is ability to hold on/cling/rely. (Rhymes–retry/strive/abide/slide)

>What one clings to doesn't matter–something noble like _____ or something ignoble like a dead baby's _____ Consider images.

>>Thrust of poem What really matters is to hold on, and so perhaps survive.

Chapter 73
MOPPING UP

Mrs Falpub straightened her hair. The staff toilet had mercifully been empty.

A drop in each eye to hide the redness.

Ready to teach–at least externally.

Chapter 74
THOUGHT

His treatment of us is that of a Father to His children—only a father infinitely more a Father than any mortal can be.

Chapter 75
TAHLA EXPOUNDS XI

Be cold! I swum swiftly...
"Hold fast that which you nab,
So that none can take your town,"
we roared.
Who? Tim who overcomes a pill.
Make like a home in the House of the Doctor.

Translation in Appendix.

Chapter 76
JOURNAL OF P ULYSSES PLUGRATH III–
ENTRY 126

'Ope springs eternal–
but you always was a sobber
of a soul, crippled at creation, blinkered at birth.
As a whelp,
he'd yelp,
and cling to his mother's knee
and trust for something better–
some hope had stirred him so.
And while he fails,
He watches a richer male
Restaurant-bound, the flail
of each wrist endemic wi'
no surrenderment of power…
It seemed once time, a young cheetah,
played and nestled at this infant's side
But now he oldens and the cat has grown–
and races pell-mell with intent in every stride.
And this rich man, replete and restaurant-tanned
Sits, power in his casual hand
The mother nearby power-filled,
commands her infant's devotion.
And I wonder
How
If these fell into such disaster
As to boggle the mind, would they know…
…know that, to survive a swirling flood,
You would grab a rich one's briefcase,
A dead baby's doll–anything to float,
Anything to survive, anything to…
…hope again?

Chapter 77
WAVES ROLL

"Come, Falpub, the book!"

"Er–it's here somewhere…" and a frantic scrabbling at bookpiles.

"You know as well as I that the journal and especially the Threat Evaluation Summary Page have to be available for access at any time by any of the civil or military authorities. The Mayor wants your book–every teacher's–now. Now, do you have it or not?"

Mrs Falpub yielded; she dare not prevaricate any longer…

"Here it is!" she cried, crossing to another pile.

The Principal flipped it open, tore out the up-to-date Threat Evaluation Summary Page, sniffed loudly–perhaps at being disappointed at the loss of how easily she had yielded–and threw the book back on the desk. "Remember your mother's continued health depends on the state's goodwill," she snarled, piercing eye catching the teacher's and then flicking away, contemptuous of what it saw. She whirled on her heel and stalked out.

Mrs Falpub collapsed into her chair, "Dear dear doctor and oh, dear love of my life, wherever you are, will this day ever curtail its pain?"

Chapter 78
THOUGHT

To find oneself as one's own individual forged through fire, and to know oneself to be internally free and strong–such is great gain.

Chapter 79
NEW ACQUAINTANCE

Third day back, and the sun shone its light down on schooldays' perpetual post-holiday dilemma. Best friends immediately connected! For all others, there was the slow elaborate dance–would a friendship forged all those eons ago (ie pre-holiday) translate unchanged? would it falter? would its Terms of Friendship be re-cast?

Alla-wuz and Tahla were back at school today. Best buds all together again! and we stood and roared our greetings at each other, while classmates rolled their eyes at the unseemliness–we only managed to bring it down a little while the Principal drifted by.

"…and I got such a bad haircut, I can hear the neck hairs scrape against my collar when I move. Listen, can you hear?"

A slight pause from the roar whilst listening carefully. Neither Alla-wuz or Tahla could hear anything, and said clearly that they couldn't.

"No, really! Listen!"–

but the conversation had already moved on. "And I'm just glow sad to be back," declared Tahla, "because I really wanted to see both of you glue knees eyes and feet. Did we eat!"

"Pardon?"

"You glue knees, eyes. You know what I said."

I worked it out. "Looney guys" had yielded "glue knees, eyes". And "feet" came from changing the first letter of "eat".

"Was Mrs Kelpub 'Franky' yesterday?"

"No, no. Mrs Falpub was alright. Sometimes she looks sad, though."

Tahla thought back to the holidays… "Twee had such a hood guy! I sent Sue a wee tide."

"OK…"

"The seaside was great! It was just Dad and me. We stepped in a lantern we got. Up early every morning! Straight away we brunched into the playcakes. Trays flew above us! I loved the crabs and sandbars. Fish, too! I brought a cream bun and ox jelly," and he rolled his eyes in disgust. "We threw that back. But every day was just as good as that. And then…" he paused dramatically, "my sack was bald."

Pause.

"You have a sack?"

Tahla looked puzzled. "Doesn't everyone? Mrs Falpub scratches hers in class. Remember?"

Back! He was talking about backs. "Your back was sore?"

He looked at me strangely. "Yes… Chad was dazing me. I stumbled, thumped hree steps, caught my foot in a stolen jam! Then I got a bald sack."

Jort came around the corner like a tidal wave walking, friends in tow on either side. The tide and its cronies surrounded me, and Alla-wuz and Tahla fled like litter carried on swirling waves.

Then they pushing me back and forth from one to the other. They daring me to stumble over feet that poked out suddenly in front of me. Curses above me like some surging hawk, waiting a chance to strike. Pushing harder, and still harder. The thump of scarcely caught balance, rasp of breath, the swirl of stairs. I heard "Teacher!" from over near the corner of the building as one of Jort's boys ran back towards us. The shoving stopped, leaving me face to face with Jort.

He punched in the stomach, hard.

I doubled over; the world seemed to have no air in it.

"Straighten up and smile, or I'll hit you again."

My hair was pulled upwards. I stood gasping, pale, smiling, world whirling.

"I'll be watching," and he and his friends fled, except for one who sat on the steps nearby, watching me.

I stood, sweat in my hair, smiling, gulping.

Alla-wuz and Tahla appeared from somewhere. "Sorry…" "So sorry…" they muttered and I smiled.

The world was whirling.

Chapter 80
RESPITE

I spent lunchtime in the library. Somehow it seemed safer.

(Alla-wuz and Tahla were absent.)

A girl approached me briefly, asked "DDDN?" but faded away quickly when I looked puzzled.

Chapter 81
JOURNAL OF P ULYSSES PLUGRATH III– ENTRY 127

When they come and we go, a group mentality, a group mind, a mind of intense acceleration and poor poor braking, where will be my strength?

I am, I am as straw before the oncoming storm and before the trampling gale. Even the great willow must bend before the tornado, before the cyclone, before the hurricane...

If I happened to believe in a higher moral being, perhaps then I might strive to choose differently, find some strength–and perhaps not be ashamed.

But I am just a straw.

Chapter 82
EVERYMAN'S CALL

I become as strength.
I (just some run-of-the-mill joe),
exist, an idea moulded in this decade's making,
Flawed but unique, I stand,
one only of my kind,
to fulfil a sighted need.
I race to pour myself out, yet to be never thirsty at the end...
I kneel to mete out strength, and to feel your strength in return...

Chapter 83
INTERLUDE

Suppose the wood in Stradivarius' forest were sentient. Some might accept him as a supreme being, their God; others may not. If believing wood were plucked from its growing place, cut with blades into long rectangular artificial shapes, taken to Stradivarius's pond and plunged into the deepest muddiest part, and held there for what seems eternity, they can give thanks that their tone, their beauty, when they are finally made into violins, will be unsurpassed for centuries. They can be content, though not perhaps happy, in their cutting, their drowning, their suffering, in what seems living death. And if the other, the unbelieving wood, should be only used as bench tables, as braces to hold the believing wood whilst it's being hewn, as paper to hold unfolding and developing ideas for a better violin, should the unbelieving wood turn to Stradivarius and say, "Treat us better and we'll believe in you!' No, the sequence has always been, "Believe in Him, be hewn of Him, and so become a violin." Without believing, there is no divine guidance for a piece of wood, no divine care for the knotty-grained twisted thing, no protection from suffering for this thing that twists and whorls and binds in on itself, no protection from the ignominies of a careless life–for just a piece of rebellious wood. How can rebellious wood claim more?

But if the rebellious wood turns, desires him, searches with all tis heart without fatigue for him, then He will be found. And then, how quickly the restoring starts, how quickly Stradivarius starts his work, despite all the imperfections, the cracks, the twisting of the years. The work begins quickly and well, all the time the wood longing for the day of the Sweetest Sound:-

Holding, yet longing to be held;
drowning, yet always beholding th'
coming light; burbling under
the waters, yet always singing.

Chapter 84
JORT SPEAKS

Look see, I'm walking down the road with me men, and life is my can of food–you try and open it and there's an unpleasant surprise, it's

One two–on the noggin,
Three four–on the floor.

Yep, I'm gonna shape my world, and the floor is part of that shape–you hit the deck willingly or you hit it with force, with the force of too much nature!! Ha! We shape our world!

So we see another gang and we're into it because there's a world watching–and back down once and they'll all know it–and our shoe is peeling back shin, our bare knuckles to their skin, and we watch them fall–we go down too, but always up and back to it– when I see one of mine on the ground and them sitting on his chest , then I over (no time like the present) and kick hard in the nose and he doubles over–and me mate from, under, like a rescue from a trap.

A shout from the road–a man in a car–and the enemy gang's scattered–me and mine are all looking cool and relaxed. He gets out–it's the local shopkeeper–and wants me in the car–so I tell the others to lose themselves–and I'm in the car all ready with my innocent blue-eyes-so-vacant look–and he says DDDN and of course I know the countersign.

"AEF,AEF," I says promptly, and he smiles and says, "Good!"

And he says, "I like your style"–he sure talks funny–and "How would you like to be in my part of the run?"

I brighten "DDDN?"

Then "yep" I says, and he gives me a place to meet, and says, "I'll drive you home"– and I sit there so proud.

I knew there always had to have been something more–and this just might be it.

It sure felt right.

Chapter 85
THOUGHT

The truth of every man is the matured potential
that once was only a seed.

Chapter 86
NEWS COMES UNEXPECTED

Flies buzzed over the evening meal, and I stood guard and chased them. The TV was on, announcing the news to any who would listen–I hoped someone else was listening, because I sure had no intention to, and my brother and sister were away...

The displayed scene shifted to a shot of the mayor sitting in the TV studio, and the words "Live Broadcast" flashed importantly at the screen's top left.

"Mayor, thank you for coming here today!"

"Always a pleasure, even in the midst of duty."

I froze, staring at the TV screen.

Sitting on the Mayor's shoulder was a snake festooned with an array of electronic gear. He blinked in and out of seeing. He sat there like an old man in a rocking chair immured by years of familiarity to just the right position (even to following all the nuances of the recliner). Comfortably he sat, then comfortably crawled through the Mayor's ear and out the other side.

The scene pulled back to show a wide shot of the studio.

"Oh Doctor, it's full of snakes," I gasped, as more upon more upon more swung into view. Draped nonchalantly on camera tripods, coiled pythonesque around cameramen's heads, rippling in and out of the walls. Sentience rippled the room in vigour.

"...and I needed this live time today to bring an important message to the people of this city..."

"Mmm?" politely prompted the announcer. And at this, the snake on his shoulder coiled itself swiftly around his head and seemed to squeeze it. As it contracted, it seemed to slip inside his head from all sides, as though skin and bone were just so much coloured fog.

"Yes, I've come for an important announcement..." and suddenly he out of his seat, to the nearest camera, and a voice suddenly bellowed from the TV.

"DDDN ... Death to the Doctor's. Death comes now. Now ... Go, go, go..."

And the TV, the house lights, the street lights all in unison went out.

Chapter 87
JENNY'S PLAYTHING

The sound of running mobs faded upwards and into hearing.

"My love, do you... The Troubles? The Genocides?" gasped Mum into Dad's ear.

"I..." Dad tilted his head, listening.

"Jenny sides?" I enquired.

Mum turned to me, a twinkle and a gasp in her eyes. "Amah, dear dear one! It's a new game–called Jenny Sides. Do you want to play?"

"Yes! Before tea?"

"Yes. Here's how we play it. You run into the thick bushes at the back of the yard"– she gestured at the shrubbery/wilderness twenty foot from the back door. "You run deep, you climb high, you hide! And if we come looking or if adults come looking, or if adults try to hunt us, it's just a game. You hide, you must not come out until we call Jenny Jenny! All out!

"If you come out before then, why there's no supper. But if you're clever and wait till the signal, there's ice-cream tonight, double ice-cream tomorrow, and triple next day. Do you like ice-cream?"

"Yes! Yes!"

"So what's the signal?"

And together we chanted 'Jenny, Jenny! All out!' with a smile on my face, and a smile and a gasp in her eyes.

"Now run, little one. Run, and remember the ice-cream!"

And up I bounded, out the door, into the shrubbery, down the frantic crawl past the bush that always flicked at my eyes as I passed, and into the thicket I had never braved before, and up and up, until I peeked out at the back door from the thickest of the shrubs.

I could clearly see Mum, see Dad, see the front door. I awaited the adventure as Mum and Dad crept together in the darkness and held each other tightly as if the large dining room was too too crowded. Seeking courage in the other's eyes, and courage in words to one far greater. Chants of a litany came to me:-

> I'm poured out like waters–
> He gathers every drop.
> I cry like a fountain–
> These tears he will store.
> They slice me as sluices–

He restores me again.
Like stars and like giants,
I'm held in his hands.

Chapter 88
WITH THE CHOIR

In the dark, thunder reached
our door.

Here

Voices that had whispered
DDDN

Here, here

Men that had kissed their
wives "Good-bye"
tenderly an hour ago

Here! Here!

they burst through our door,
corporate, mechanised,
a unit. A human muscle
knowing their job.

Here, here I come with a baseball bat

Legs that had once run to
play Catch with their children
pounded like a chain gang
into the room, ready
to work.
Minds that had laughed or
saddened or reflected just
twenty-four hours ago

Here I come with a baseball bat,
Been idle all

moved as one, part of
the unit.

Here I come with a baseball bat,
Been idle all day, and ready

at the back of a mind,
perhaps a doubt… But
this was big, this was
venting, this was
testosterone on speed,
this was a battalion, here
was the mission

> *Here I come with a baseball bat,*
> *Been idle all day, and ready to whack*
> *See it rise, see you fall*
> *So obedient t' gravity's call.*

Steel hands grabbed the middle-aged beings before them, one male, one female. While one turned to turn the dead TV's volume to maximum, pumping muscle obeying adrenalin and directions coming from behind deadened eyes moved them like a steam train into the backyard.

> *Once more! With feeling!! Right?*
> *Now!*
> *Here I come with a baseball bat,*
> *Been idle all day, and ready to whack*
> *See it rise, see you fall*
> *So obedient t' gravity's call.*

Snake-controlled beings hurled the weaker duo to the ground; and
lay
stood irresolute, amazed at how even despised entities could yield so easily
lay me down
to the naked muscle.
lay me down. rest
A glimmer from behind ten eyes that this was big
lay me down. Rest in seeing—
Night-time
Ten eyes thought this unusual, they were violating the inviolable.
lay me down. Rest in seeing—
Night-time flickers. Pain is beating.
Ten eyes thought that hands that had held wives shouldn't be here. Then a drowning under the corporate will…
lay me down. Rest in seeing—
Night-time flickers. Pain is beating.

Breaks
of kicks, of punches, of sticks rising and falling.
lay me down. Rest in seeing–
Night-time flickers. Pain is beating.
Breaks a day where peace is

lay me down. Rest in seeing–
Night-time flickers. Pain is beating.
Breaks a day where peace is ever

Lay me down. Rest in seeing–
Night-time flickers. Pain is beating.
Breaks a day where peace is ever,
Holds the Doctor and I'm the victor.

The mother of all explosions shrieked! A flashing, a roaring of flares sprawled–lit up the sky like shards of candy cane gone insane. Startled beast eyes looked up from blood on the ground at a sky wrong, a sky now flickering and waving red, at a sky which reflected explosions from far away.

The TV spluttered to life. The mayor's voice boomed out from a thousand television sets in a thousand houses, each having been turned on by an invading mob:-

"The gas mains, you fools.. They've all gone up. Put out the fires, leave the people! Put out the fires, or we're all gone!"

And a sudden evacuation of snakes from startled eyes, a pounding, a running. And perhaps tomorrow a cringing, a crying, a shame-facedness that could swing instantly either to repression or further violence in an instant.

Chapter 89
THE JOURNEY

The fear was there, but small compared with the need for action and with the certainty of a bigger Doctor. The small one could chose to ignore the fear, and so he raced, hand upon twist, clamber upon wriggle, full of action, out from the shrubbery towards them, keeping his mind on the action.

Still, fear lurked like the smell of an alien landscape. It lurked, but receiving no attention, it slowly closed in, starved itself, died.

I reached them, throat gasping over tears.

"Mum … Dad…."

They both moved…

Both held me.

Chapter 90
JOURNAL OF P ULYSSES PLUGRATH III–
ENTRY 128

Born into times too big for me,
Near strongmen henchmen too fierce for me.
Like a wheel without brakes, I'm driven, driven…
I roll, I roll…

Que

sera

sera…

Chapter 91
AFTERMATH

He coiled around the medal. Tongue licked at it with satisfaction–inhaled its scent.

He'd won again! The award ceremony this morning had also yielded a plaque, and he levitated to where it poised on the wall of their hidden craft as it nestled between trees, and read it again:-

To Adder Company

125

Greg and Kathy Weller

Congratulations on your erudition
in
using subterfuge to facilitate civil war
at a time when such tactics are
widely considered ineffective.
A job well done."

And he bounced around the cabin, content for the first time in (it almost seemed like) an epoch.

Chapter 92
ANOTHER MATH

As we returned home from the hospital, dawn kissed a smoky haze, and Dad walked to the house slowly. His crutch creaked in a hugging fog, and some of our neighbours looked and stared. We had been the first house—and consequently the only house—in our street to be hit.

The quiet staring grated. I felt like an animal pinned and examined.

Then inside the house and click the door.

Inside my mind, the hugging fog continued. ...

Chapter 93
MINUS THE ONE

Tahla came over later. I was sort of half-glad when he left.

Chapter 94
JOURNAL OF P ULYSSES PLUGRATH III–
ENTRY 129

Supermarket laden …. then I stumbled onto that family. The father with the bandaged leg and crutch…

My hands in that blood!–a jagged thought lightning across the mind, then stifled.

I so wanted to not look, and yet to look to see if they recognized me… The shuffly eye patterns must look strange.

But no recognition in his eyes–I'm sure of it. The woman too looked right through me.

Pretty thing…

The kid–I saw no kid on the night, but he stared at me with round eyes, jerking at his mother's hand, not to attract her, but just twitching motions of young kids when they don't know what to do.

He had round eyes like pools of liquid guilt.

I stumbled to the next aisle, and didn't see them again there.

Those feelings–such an interesting kaleidoscope!.

And probably useful for a poem

After the intensity subsides.

Chapter 95
MRS FALPUB REMEMBERS

I've lost him.

Days spent hand in hand near the Doctor, an argument, a leaving. And now gone, life snuffed out last night–it was on the TV.

Lost. We never … but in bed last night, I felt so cold, cold a brick in my heart, another twist in the throat, eyes crying steel ball bearings of tears–they hurt too much upon their generation to have been water–ball bearings of sorrow from a heart made anarchist…

His photograph–shattered frame. I threw him in anger to the other side of the room. He's broken. Tear in half the picture, and lost.

Chapter 96
JOURNAL OF P ULYSSES PLUGRATH III–
ENTRY 130

So proud!

Wrote a poem–amazing what lunch can do for you! Here it is!

> I see you and I walk
> To talk with you, potential good friend
> And hugging one. And we
> Talk a little, nothing deep
> And inside I pleasure like a small child
> Contented there, but aware and alert
> For pain can razor happiness and
> Sorrow cuts through joy.
> And I hold the mirror to myself
> And see it shattered; shards
> shower my feet
> And as I pick up each one
> Written on them I read,
> "Mum and Dad didn't like each other when
> I was young, but they get on OK now."
> (savage glass). And, "My girlfriend's leaving.
> He moves; he woos. My hands so clumsy,
> I don't know what to do."
> Another jags, "I'll go out with Jo, cause
> I'm better than her, and so
> Can handle the deal." But another
> Found later: "I can't handle ... Jo."
> But we talk and smile, and I sadly walk away
> Because, inside, I really would like to stay.

Not bad for a first draft anyway! Might as well put up the bod on the bed and have a sleep before dinner.

And anyhow, maybe if I hadn't gone out last night, I may not have been able to write that poem.

Chapter 97
ALLA-WUZ REMEMBERS THE BULLY

I'm so sorry, my friend–that bullied day, I ran, cried inside.

With ears and trunk aflare with blushing, I stumbled round the corner, I and Tahla, and stood trembling, not meeting each other's eyes, sledgehammers lying restless on our tongues while you faced the tidal wave alone.

Once when I was younger, in kindergarten, the kids came, the others, the ones who looked like you–no nose, no ears with potatoes–and they started with names: Trunky Skunk and Yellow Guts.

Later, they would pick up a potato that had dropped from behind my ears and threw it hard at my back. I could never turn around when they hit, scared of how large a crowd might be behind me...

And one day, two came as friends. "Alla-wuz," they said, "can you make a figure eight with your trunk?" When I proudly showed them, they pulled it tight and tighter until it hurt, and I screamed until the adults came. It ached for days after...

I look at you and I see me.

I looked around the corner then and saw you pushed and shoved, and I tasted sledgehammer.

And I know that on Fire Night, they came. To you and yours they came–I heard noise from my house, and I felt figure-eights.

Friendship has writhed like grass in the fire and now there is only fear this minute.

In this second of knotting, in this instant of piercing thorns.

Chapter 98
QUICK NOW

"Today is a new day," I declared to the spider eyeing me balefully. He crouched in the corner of my room, while I sprawled on my belly, elbows on the floor, head on my hands. The spider seemed unsure of the large monster speaking to him–after all, he had no venom, just bluff. So he bluffed, rocking back on his back legs, front legs raised and threatening. The monster seemed unimpressed.

"Today I'm going to be good friends again with Alla-wuz and Tahla, and I'm going to live quietly, not be hateful at anyone, and I'll work hard again at school. Everything will work out, you'll see."

The spider flailed its forehands, then seeing the monster was fearless, backed away uncertainly.

And entering the kitchen, I found Dad had given away his crutch for a light walking stick. "Hello, sleepyhead. How would you like to take a walk to the newsagent before breakfast?"

My eyes were round. ."...before breakfast?"

"Yeah, well, we would have waited till after breakfast, but you took so long to wake up." Dad winked at Mum, who tried to wink back. The bruise on her face was darkening into two patches.

"I'll be back!" and I dashed upstairs, into suitable clothes and shoes, and out again, the spider also having left earlier.

I bounced along the street beside Mum and Dad, exuberance and two stable rock-like structures together. Dogs strained to self-mutilate themselves against leashes, birds rejoiced, and dew fell upwards as our feet passed. I dashed to a swing, had three back-and-forths, then onto the kerb edge, balancing and walking on its edge, and raced to the corner and back in the time it took Mum and Dad to pass one house.

I calmed myself as we entered the newsagent.

Mum went to the newspaper rack. I stared at the small toy cabinet, imagining what it would be like to own it all, and Dad looked around for the large rack of books about the Doctor. It had moved down near the back, into an ill-lit corner, but Dad and I made for it. Even some of Tahla's writings had made it onto the stand.

As we reached it, there seemed to be a loud hiss. Startled, both Dad and I looked around, but could see no-one that it could have been. Everyone was absorbed in their paper, their book, their magazine–although it seemed one man's hand shook slightly, rustling his paper.

Nevertheless, Dad found a book and took it to the shopkeeper, who took his money in stony silence. The room seemed gritty with hate as we turned to leave.

Behind, someone called, "Burnt any good cities lately?" and then a silence.

We walked, looking straight ahead, ears vibrating. *Why do eardrums vibrate at instants of sudden stress* crossed my mind. And the trip home seemed much longer. There was a holding of hands and a quick pulling away in deference to some internal pain, and then another re-seeking of contact. House windows gaped vacantly at us, unsure of what emotion to reflect. Finally we reached the path to our house, and something beckoned with a homely smell.

I ran up the path to the front stair, also putting my foot into the small fire burning up a few sticks and rubbish. Alongside, someone had written on the wall with the end of a burnt stick

and next?

Behind our backs, the street looked sleepy, pristine, untouched.

In; bolt; lock the door. Half-mutters for communication.

And each to his own brooding–if grief has a heart, its name is loneliness.

And I sat and trembled. Mum sat quietly and read some of Tahla's writings, and presently her breathing slowed.

Dad went to the spare room, and I heard a dull thump, pause, dull thump.

I had to see...

I peeked around the corer to see Dad moving in triple-quick time, lifting furniture (his leg somehow holding out), then moving the furniture, dumping nuisance stuff in the hall. He gave a quick smile to me. "I've said for two years this room had to be re-arranged, and today's the day to do it!"

He turned away and triple-quick-time-work continued.

I went and sat near Mum trying to ignore the dull thump, pause, dull thump, louder thump. Presently I said to Mum, "What's wrong with Dad?"

"It's just his way of dealing with a shock. He works hard and fast so he can forget it."

"Oh."

I listened for a while. The thump pause thump seemed to be getting even faster.

"Mum, I don't like it. Make him stop."

"Hush, dear one .... come here," and she cuddled me, she with bruises on her face, me feeling like I had some too. And comfort came.

Nearby, the newspaper lay unread.

Chapter 99
JORT STEPS UP

"You really should not have bought the boy along. The Mayor supports us, but really!.. . there are departments in his office he has to at least pretend to listen to."

He inhaled through a comfort-accustomed nose (thus enjoying the limousine's new car smell), adjusted a hand-stitched tie; indolence was in his fingertips and charm lurked in his smile. "So why, dear friend, do you want to push us into futility, thereby wasting all our efforts to date?"

"The boy has it in him. I saw him walk up to a kneeling kid and in cold blood, kick his nose so hard I heard the crack 30 feet away."

A short pause, then hurry on, "And when I called out and ran towards them, he stayed– ready to convince me black was white, or that I had not really seen what I saw, or . . . I don't know what. Guts, hunger and ice–that's what I saw."

"OK. Make him the video camera boy if you must–but he's not to get involved in the violence. That's it!"

And comfort departed in powder and exhaust fumes.

Chapter 100
UN-SEEKING ALLIES

If someone is the scene of the accident, they're the one obsessed by it–surely!

The solution was simple:- I wouldn't go to school–even going outside the front door was perilous, and my stomach flipped and twisted like a landed fish looking for safety.

"Mum, I think I'm going to chuck," and the possibility did lurk in the background– something elusive, but... She looked at me thoughtfully, her hand absentmindedly tracing the bruise on her face from that night. She ran her cool mother hand across my brow. The intrusive detection hovered for a moment, then declared essential soundness of health.

I seethed.

"And for firsts, your breakfast," declared the long-haired torturer.

...and I did. Sullenly.

Later, in my room, hiding my school clothes, I changed into the darkest, blackest clothes I could find. Creeping downstairs to the dim black space behind the washing machine, I nestled into the dusty niche, and waited. Though adrenalin coursed in veins and palms sweated with tension, I strove for stillness.

Time defied me and slowed down.

An agony of eternity later, I heard the late morning noises—the ones that always preceded my going to school. The clipping of Dad's bag, his last-minute trip to the toilet. Any moment now, the saying of goodbyes, the assumings I had already left for school...

"Dear, have you seen the lad? His school port's still here."

Blast, I'd forgotten that.

Next came the sound of searchings approaching, some implacable steam train towards its victim. The sweat on my hands became clammy then was covered by fresh outpourings from the pores. Hair stuck to the sweat on my head but I dared not move. Mum appeared, staring into my hiding place, one arm holding herself up on the ledge above me. We stared at each other. I dared not move, we stared, and then she stood up, hand running along the dusty ledge. "I don't know," she sighed, and walked away.

Even in the flurry of dust, I found time to sigh with relief, then sneezed vigorously.

The footsteps re-approached, eyes looked—and this time, they saw.

"Hello, dear. Going to school today?"

That was a question to which No invited danger, I decided. "Yes, yes, of course."

"Come on out then, and we'll get ready."

This time, Mum helped me dress, fussed, loved . . . but was always in the room. "You know, dear," she said, breaking the long silence. "The Doctor is always with us and we can talk to him about anything. Anything at all."

That was easy talk. She could stay forever in this house—there was no Jort in her life. And I couldn't tell her—not now, not ever. So "Mmm..."

Dressing and grooming done, she stood up and eyed me judiciously. "And today, I'll pick you up from school, and we'll go out and eat, just us two."

I brightened. This was good news.

So she drove me to school, and I waved bye furtively before entering the grounds.

Chapter 101
JOURNAL OF P ULYSSES PLUGRATH III–
ENTRY 138

"Well, I'm racing down the track.
Aint no looking back
And I'm pressing the attack
'Gainst the Doctor and his pack.
Don't you know we're going to
Give them a broken neck."

Does this reflect the feeling accurately? Am I getting to like it?

Chapter 102
SUGAR TEARS

Mum's bruise has changed to scabs running in a long line down her face in two long trails–as if she put treacle high in two places and let it run unabluted and never ever cleaned it.off.

Dad gets a horrified glazed expression whenever Mum kisses him, and still has bouts of triple-quick fever.

Following the Doctor is so much pain.

Chapter 103
UN-SEEKING I

Alla-wuz asked me to play at his house today, but I said I had to get home.
Don't care much for Tahla either...

Chapter 104
UN-SEEKING II

They want to send me to my aunt in the country.
Why can't I stay here??

Chapter 105
UN-SEEKING III

I saw Mum hit Dad today. Then the neighbour took me away.
I think I'm screaming.

Chapter 106
ALLA-WUZ MISSES

The early train hoots its siren and I half-raise my head and drop it back on the pillow, so my ear folds back and a potato rolls away. Hitting the floor it bounces once, twice, then rolls, more well-behaved, to its chosen destination.

The blanket prickles my leg, and so I angrily flip it to one side, then think better of it and adjust it more accurately with my nose.

The hour till daylight stretches like an eternity of cyclic pain. I had been through this loop and through it again, and still my mind traces its circuit down the well-worn path. I went there today, he said he doesn't feel like getting together, looks at me with a half-glazed expression, and shuts the door.

After all our years of best buds, there is only, "I don't want to. Bye."

Sure his house had been broken into–I could see the nails hammered into the splintered door frame to hold it secure–but no one was really hurt....

Glazed expression, bye...

It's not been the same since Tahla. He can't talk properly, can't write properly, and I up, determined to outdo the fool.

Take a saying, change it into something else. Come on, where's the art in that?

Take a saying...

A good deed never goes unrewarded now.

Swap the second, third and second last vowels around; manipulate the sounds. There–changed!

A gourd, dude, never goes unreweeded now

Not half bad! Eat your heart out, Pepper Boy!

No wait, something better–swap the consonants too!

A gnawed dude never roars, "Knee needed! Now!!"

There, message from the Dr said in a silly way because of brain damage.

Oh dear! Insurrective me. A mock smack on the backside, and back into bed, a yawning chasm between me and old friends.

Satisfied! To sleep, to sleep.

And in the half-drift, I thought I saw a golden seam along my arm, and something pointed weave its slithering line along the seam, whispering, "Open, please. Please open…" and then I fell asleep.

Chapter 107
TUMBLE FROM DEPRESSION

A quick tumbling to the knees, a hurt wet with tears.

A praying, "Doctor, I need you to survive the battle, the forces against me. But just don't ask me to forgive the torturers in my town…."

An easier breathing, comfort by Aider, a knowing that violence is not an option for the Doctor's believers, a rising, a getting on with things.

Chapter 108
TUMBLE, AS PARENTS, FROM DEPRESSION

HE   Waves lapped at me today, and I was scared,
Waves of doubt promised their ability to wear down,
And I was afraid.
So when you were suddenly there, snarling in your hurt,
It was too much, and I, from the top of my shaky rock,
Reacted, moved as if to strike.
And I'm sorry.
I had always seen myself as a man living
atop a solid and vast rock in the midst
of a desolate waste,
and it shakes me to the core that doubt has come.
Waves have poured over the desert;
have tumbled down off the low long rocks,
making cascades, hugged tightly the rock
at my core, and climbed, caressing. They
have pressured the grip,
have pressured, edging
higher and higher.

Have you pondered such pressure as water?
Divers, we hear,
suffer from its play, its thrumming,
its pushing down, the compression,
the diminution of gases. And I
never knew until these past weeks
the pressure of many waters
on the base, on my core,
until now.
And it feels in every way as if
all of my foundations erode,
have eroded, will erode,
will be crumbling.
And were I to lose you, you! because
of my hurt, my agony, all
that was green (or all that
you had taught to become green)
around my rock,
or in the trees in the crevices,
in the grass hugging the level
flataways on this vast and lonely
rock, would die,
would wither straightways.
Kissed with too much sun
that strikes with savage intensity
its UV, they would flee—and
I, too, would run from the sun,
seek a darkest corner of desolation,
and be.
Tumbled over by hurt,
by despair,
by hopelessness,
I could only . . .
exist,
trembling and shredded inside...

SHE   I have poured forth children for you from my loins,
      Have lived for them, for you, for the structures that are ours.

And in my rage at the Doctor, and what I saw as impotent arms,
I cursed Him … aloud … and I cursed you inside my heart.
When I hunt, I am as if a cat,
Bristles all agog, all at attention.
I walk, I bustle through narrow spaceways
And what once fitted around me now scrapes bristled hairs
And th' fur yells to me. From all directions it yells
That all is not right, that it must be rectified,
Lanes must be straightened, must be widened–But how?
It comes from all around, so I cannot move this way or that.
And so I panic, I strike out in any direction at anything pliant,
Anything which might give way, might yield.
Room, room, I must have room!
And in this hill,
In this fetid stinking morass of mangrove,
Of sump pump gone wrong,
The only soft things I found were the Doctor, the son, and you.
And I strike, and I struck, and thus had struck for
A past vast eternity (two weeks) at all of you, at any of you.
As time jagged on, as time tumbled as broken glass down,
Down over my trembling naked body
Twirled up in foetal position,
I have snarled, I have… I'm sorry.

HE   Come, hold me.

SHE   Your breath is warm, dear. I had almost forgotten…

HE   And yours

And presently they kissed once.
And again.
And again, with feeling

Chapter 109
THE WANDERERS' BATTLE

"We must needs pass over the mountain pass separating the two valleys." So up and up we strode. The company being good, the day passed quickly. And then fell the night.

We arose in the morning as ice clinked and dripped in the trees, somewhat short on temper and even shorter on sleep. But still, the chill soon fled before the morning sun, and we soon reached the crest, and looked on the fertile valley below. The villagers as ants bustled busily, and we again were soon telling tales of honour earnt by distant friends on alien shores. (The Lattice promoted (within my emotional framework) joy of bravery and striving for honour simultaneously, diminishing my uncertainty within this opening scene.)

Floating slightly askew to the ground and to my right, I noticed a thin glow rippling mid-air. The thinness solidified swiftly, until resembling a man-shaped bottle–and still it glowed.

Beside it another thin glow rippled.

"Gedathel, behold!"

"Still! It is the extrudants." Swift as thought, he drew his great sword and sliced through the three shining ripples. They punctured like worn waterskins, and a loathsome evil-smelling fluid oozed to the ground–then was absorbed into it with a prolonged hiss.

"The extrudants have found us, old friend. The battle is soon here." He swept his keen sight across the peaceful pastoral scene, then pointed in the direction of our so-recent ascent. There a score of bottles glowed green under the shadows of the trees. And over to our right they also festooned, numbers such as fill a warrior's heart with joy and yet foreboding.

Then as a bottle filling up with liquid, colour, with shape, a living being poured into each simultaneously, and they were upon us. And yet, beyond their shoulders, more green ripples danced.

And we turned, Gedathel and I, to the battle, our backs together, he with two glittering great swords such as only he could wield, and I, mallet-handed and with a crossbow that was always primed. We strove together in the bucolic land, strove in bitterness of spirit against those who would take our lands, our wives, all hope, would take all lives.

The roar of the horde, the roar of Gedathel, he of the two swords, and the rapid twang twang of the crossbow, the cry of the fallen enemy (their green falling into the grass), the smell like a myriad crushed roaches at the passing of each, the wielding of the mallet for those who would circle from the side, the sweat of Gedathel's back against mine, the shifting of feet, the striking down of the enemies, the thrusting and withdrawing of the great swords from fractured green sides, the fatigue that hovered at the corners of our eyes, that tugged unbidden at muscles that must needs discharge their duty, the stinging of sweat in our eyes, the holding, the faithful keeping of each our watches.

Gedathel and I laboured completing our charge, our appointed call. Then the rippling of green in the air, the pouring forth of an extrusion of Hirmwhet (the traitor, the great enemy). The traitor's smirk as he turned, as he turned with a great sword spinning nimbly in a doubly-jointed wrist, and the roaring of Gedathel as he saw the traitor and rushed forward, forsaking me, and the tumbling down of Gedathel from an extrudant knave's blow to his exposed back, and then the fall and the fall and the

And Gedathel lay prone, the knave over him raising a sword, razor sharp, never before having felt the cutting of human flesh. And the raising, the base savage joy of the knave, the nameless pit in my stomach.

And I turning, turning, to aim my bow…

But lo! The battle call, the charge from the trees of a new face, the striking of the extrudant as he hesitated between the fallen quarry and the new threat.

And with a roar, my crossbow rising. Crossbow moving … and the arrow away.

And the villain fell, splashing green over Gedathel. The new figure reached Gedathel, raised him to his feet with one hand—whilst with practiced skill cutting away the life from two of the enemy.

Then the forming of we three back to back as a triangle of life, fending against the fallen green things which kept coming.

Or so we thought, for at the swelling of our numbers, they lost heart quickly and disappeared into green ripples, leaving we three on a green-drenched hillside beneath a sun daring to peek, to touch, to warm the hearts both of warriors and of those whom they protect.

Thus presently, crossbow dropped, great swords yielded to gravity, the adrenalin faded to bone-heaviness, and we turned to the sudden rescuer, who even now removed his battle helmet. And the word "Father" tore from Gedathel's throat.

They embraced, father and son, re-united. And Gedathel cried before the listening heavens. "Truly today you are more than my father. For once you gave life to me—and today you have given life again. More than a father—indeed a father from heaven you have become."

And they embraced with tears. .

Chapter 110
TUMBLING–IN

I'm back home!!
Mum and Dad are better. They kiss each other in front of me all the time.
They shut their door at night and giggle to each other. Where do they find the jokes??
Maybe it's going to be OK.
I think I'll find Alla-wuz again very soon.

Chapter 111
JORT SPEAKS II

So the little kid–the one who rides norses–walks into the trap. He walks along the second storey landing at just the regular time, and all of an instant there's one of my men at his side, just back a little so the boy speeds up. He's off balance, see. (Get the mind spinning and every blow hits a little heavier, every imagined cut slices nearer the bone.)

And at the instant the mind feels vulnerable for the first time, suddenly a second at the other side, appearing in an instant from a classroom door, and the boy speeds up. And he starts expecting action, so the men start to speak, so he's off balance, each speaking a word so his mind darts from side to side, seeking escape, but we're always there–and they talk back and forth about how to hurt him–one word, one word, one word

I	We
think	could
we	trip
could	him
hit	hit
him	his
in	head
the	against
head	the
No	wall
I	You're
think	right
that	this

And so, and so...

And the sweat appears on him, and a third comes from behind, and instantly there's one on each side and one at the back up against him tight and walking fast, so he's skidding and they're breathing the words

"and kill"

"and kill"

"and kill"

and he trembles a little—and suddenly I'm in front of him just at the top of the stairs.

And I looks at him sternly and tell him to smile—they're still coming towards me quick, him skidding, and he tries a smile, and I call "wider" and he does it wider, the first "smile" so inside him he knows he's a coward, and then to make him smile wider, so he knows there's no doubt of it.

And as they reach me at the top of the stairs, the one at the side steps back, and I push him hard, and he's down the stairs two at a time, three at a time, spinning, and he calls out, "Doctor, help!" And I call DDDN and my men echo AEF AEF, and we're away except one, who sits at the top of the stairs and watches as he staggers away.

Always let him know evil is near...

Chapter 112
PEELING BACK TO SINGLENESS

No one helps, no one can be there. Alla-wuz and Tahla weren't there, never have been there to help me with Jort. Mum and Dad themselves bowed down as defiant flowers before the bullies.

Yet, at the end, we three, Mum and Dad and I, beaten but not crushed, have hung in there...

I have called to the Doctor, and there was help! Even the writings encourage me!

In the fire, only the Doctor is Other enough to be there with me.

I raise my hands to no violence,
My God raises his hands to keep.

Chapter 113
THE BETTER UNDERWEAR

The good feeling from earlier has worn off. Jort looks like a pestilence at the back of rats' throats, full-formed, virulent, waiting to strike.

But I must remember that in the stress, there is the calling out; in the amazement that this is happening to me, there is the Doctor as strong tower; in my desire to bargain, there is only a need to bargain with the One who loves me; and when I accept the situation, it is only because the Doctor wants me here.

I wear the situation and emotions as a jumper—the underwear supplied by faith in the Doctor.

I sleep at night, for you are there.
I awake in the morning
for you have sustained me.

Chapter 114
JORT SPEAKS III

So I say to my men my new motto
Disassembly required—with finesse.
Not like the DDDN mob—they hit with sticks; they forget what to do when the victim is reeling; they back off saying, "We'll be back tomorrow. Change your ways!" ...when just a twist at the twenty-fifth second of the cycle, and the idiot would be goobering into their shoes, or into the foetal position in silent scream.

They won't shape their victim's world. One sits and writes poetry wallowing in self-pity. And there's no time like the present—my present, my new present—and as for the victim, their first moulding or their final shaping or collapsing (whichever's first)!

Hey it's good to shape with art.

Chapter 115
ALLA-WUZ TUMBLES INTO DEPRESSION, MEETS "THE POWDER"

He walked into the small retail concern, his powder wafting gently through his nostrils, entering the nasal cavity, playing gently with the pheromone detection mechanisms there. Endorphins triggered benevolent goodwill, and he smiled at an ordered world he had helped create.

Down and to the serving counter, there to meet with an entry-level clerk who would show appropriate respect, submission, genufecture of being.

...but no, not yet. There, scarcely past the level of his well-muscled thigh, with muscled quadriceps and glutes that had helped kick in heads in his youth, and now trained others in how to do it, was a small mammal, large-eared, prehensile nose—and learned rage flooded his being. He felt the discomfort of deeper breathing as the greater degree of inhaling drove powder a little too quickly towards the nasal receptors, felt the faster diastolic and systolic rhythm associated with encountering a world not sufficiently trained as yet, and the slight sweat within the creases of his palms scared, troubled him.

Still, appropriate restraint before the general populace. So, just a gruff, "You should go away boy... I can help you go away," and a satisfied onrush within the cerebral networks as the young eyes looked startled into his.

But no! the look of respect in the young eyes turned to rage, and a step back, and a half charge, a wrapping of the nose around his waist, a squeezing, a paining, a slight extruding of the relaxed muscle sheet of the abdominal cavity above and below the structure so as to form a three-inch swelling on either side of the tightening object. And could that be? a whisper escaped his mouth, a slight flexing of the phalanges in strong immediate discomfort, and an eternity of a minute of self-doubt and of the doubt of continued existence under this temporal pain.

The easing as he tumbled to his knees, the consequent moisture of the water gathering in the creases of his hands and forehead. The charge in odour of the powder as excess bodily waste poured through sweat glands, the staring at the aggressor.

"Now, learn to respect others!" trumpeted the miniature powerhouse before him, and it turned to leave. He knew the look on the young face—a look familiar: a look of satisfaction that the other had learnt the lesson, had accepted second status, had learnt respect.

Out the door, and silence.

Adrenalin, now in overabundance in his body through unexpected aggression called, seeking a new goal, then surged powerfully in the rage that emanated from the brain. Signals poured to heart, to eyes, to nostrils flaring, to upper and lower peripherals, to their extremities, met the adrenalin, combined in a fervent heady mix of rage, power, and need for revenge.

A calling out, "Tell your mama to keep you safe, boy, ," a hasty retreat, an entry to the limousine, the tickling of the powder over his breathing service as the adrenalin drove the respiratory mechanism still far too quickly.

A need for revenge, a need to see submission.

Chapter 116
AMAH, UNDER THE ARC, STANDS ABOVE THE ARC

I bound down the street, I alone. Who needs friends . . . Tahla and he across the road, past items, discarded issues, rank reminders of a different me. They at school, and I here alone, at the arc of the day.

Reach the zebra crossing. Look both ways–don't you know that mama taught me well–and across.

Halfway across, I look at the other side, to see . . . Jort. Like me, wagging school–unlike me, he sits like a mushroom cloud, smiles like a energetic cheetah having detected an easy bull, sits watching.

His eyes travel to my feet, my hands as they slow. I stand in the midst of the crossing looking at rainclouds with thunder, and they become something to avoid, to seek the better component of valour, to withdraw strategically from the potential trouble spot, and I turn, gracefully seek relief on the side of the street I had so recently left.

But hold . . . there waiting at road edge, another assassin's face, a smile from comic books, and my feet pause.

Perched high on the arc of the road I stand, like a troubled stranded flood victim, danger on every side.

Startled, I look up as a car, a long car, turns the slight bend in the road before me. A speeding up as they see me, a revving, almost playful, of the engine. Jaw drops, nose drops, and astonishment plays with my mind. To me, this can't be happening to me.

The car seems to get wider, the engine revving, closer, the sun catches the chrome in an instant, blinds me for a split second, thoughts spill through my head something about moving, but there's no time, no time, time has fled.

The car goes into a slow screeching; time races in slow motion to inevitable consequences. The hitting...

The hitting will come soon, and thoughts spill in the head searching for nerve pathways to find the legs, but there's no time, and...

The car jerks as it comes to a halt, the brakes finally finding their mark. I gawp, knowing that I gawp, knowing the brain has found its way to my legs which have started to tremble.

Water has formed on the road between them.

The window comes down, a small piece of paper is waved from it, Jort races, grabs it, brings it to me, smiling, an almost dreamy look in his eyes. I smell powder . . . somehow familiar.

I read, words forcing themselves as water through cracks in a frozen mind, forming puddles of meaning, coalescing into paragraphs of intent.

"Didn't I tell you, boy, to ask your mama to watch you. Jort has been authorised to teach you how to respect."

And I look up–dreamy dreamy look in Jort's eyes–the reversing of the long car away and down a side street–the moving towards me of Jort's second–the screeching around the corner of a police car–their pulling up to houses nearby, their exiting the car, entering the house's yard, knocking on the door–their pausing and waiting.

I look around, Jort and second back quietly, casually on the footpath, still smiling at me, and I turn to find home again, thankfully only a short sharp distance of rapid steppings away.

Chapter 117
FORCE

I scurried away from school! Mum hadn't come to pick me up, and I had to be home to watch my TV show.

Oblivious to the dog barking on the corner, I turned into the long stretch.

It was blocked.

Grabbed from behind, I felt a cloth bag dragged over my head. My hand pushed up to remove it but I heard Jort's voice.

"Stay still."

And I froze.

"Now smile," and inside my bag, I smiled

He couldn't see me, I thought, the bag is black, but I couldn't risk it . . .

"Wider . . . "

Sweat came. He could see, truly! How could he have known? I smiled to split my face.

"Not good enough," and a push came from the direction in which I could hear breathing. And I fell hard against a fence.

"Up now, up now."

Somehow I found my feet, my balance.

A hit with the ferocity of a norse, and I was down, and weight pressing on my chest.

"Give it me"—Jort's voice, sounding very close.

"What do you want?" I asked trembling.

"Not you. You can't give me nothing, except pain."

And water poured down on my face through the mask.

I held my breath until my world spun. I strove. I strove to hold.

I strove. I opened my mouth, gasping. Water poured in.

I swallowed—too much, too much!

And "I'm going to die," twitched across my mind, and I remembered the Doctor who held—held while the body with its life force bucked and struggled.

Then it stopped. The water stopped.

Then the fists started, muddled and slipped on the cloth bag, but found their goal right enough.

Pain leached into white light.

Chapter 118
LEACHED LITANY

I'm poured out like waters–
He gathers every drop.
I cry like a fountain–
These tears he will store.
They slice me as sluices–
He restores me again.
Like stars and like giants,
I'm held in his hands.

Chapter 119
GREY AND WHITE

A fist pounded into my eye and lights flew everywhere.

The lights lingered, held, bathed me. "It's wrong, it's all wrong. Too light. It can be this much light," jagged across my mind.

I opened my eyes. The light continued.

I could dimly see a tree near me, white, bleached white, swimming in light.

Moving my head, I saw white grass. I grabbed at it, and it cut my hand. "Just my luck," I thought, "swordgrass!"

Blood leaked out pale.

Above me was a shadow, and a hand reached down.

Bones gripped my skin-over-bones and pulled me up.

The light ebbing, I saw a grey . . . person in front of me. Blank mirrors for eyes reflected by bloodied self.

"Come boy, you'll need to get home."

"Where am I? Is home near here?"

The grey one blinked his eyes once and tut-tutted.

"Much preponderance to prevaricate in self-imposed hallucinations."

"Pardon?"

"You daydream too much. 'Non-diligent defence delves into defeat' as the saying goes."

"I daydream?"

"Your species in general. One quarter daydream too much, the remainder spend time plotting violence." And he tut-tutted again.

Then, "Home, boy. You know the way. Utilise legs like a toolchest."

I looked, the light having faded, and there I was, in the street. An age ago, I was under a mass of fists and hate.

"Who are you, sir?"

"I've come to watch out for you and your friends."

"Why? Why would you come?"

"Your group is important, as they say, to 'fight to the other side of the nova'."

"Important?"

He snorted angrily. "Pre-occupation with irrelevant dilemmas are counter-productive and injurious to continued preservation." Then he blinked and calmed. "Go on home, boy, or they 'll be back. OK?"

"OK . . ."

I ran home. At the corner of the street, I looked back. I saw the small grey man walk into a craft which had suddenly appeared, gave him entrance, then disappeared again.

"A UFO, an alien. . ." I gulped.

Chapter 120
HOUSE CALL

I was pondering my meeting with the grey when there was a knock at my door.

I opened it to see Jort.

"I'm in," he said and suddenly he was standing in my living room.

"We gotta talk," he said.

Chapter 121
JORT SPEAKS IV

And I remember this kid–I'm sitting in his chair, but I'm remembering somewhere else.

I had been sitting, shaping this kid's world–moulding his being through terror–had easily blinded him then down to the ground and I'm sitting there, knees pressing into his upper arms, and my men give me water, and it's over over his nose and mouth steady (like the water that wears down too), and some of it goes in, gets in him.

It's nothing much–just a moment of truth to see what bubbles out of his soul:- it may be anger, maybe pain, but he's never the same after, and there's my world a little better. And there's his world shaped.

Hey! He'll never look at me the same again!

And I was there slowly taking apart his head to re-build–the deconstruction then the re-construction–and suddenly

a great roar

and the sky falls to white

and we hear a voice, "In the Name of the Doctor" and we run–my men head over tail and out of there. Ha, running like we was being shaped, hey?

And the kid I was shaping–I'm sitting here in his building now. Just us, and he's talking He says its an alien, not the Doctor–but, . . . I see that if you got someone like that alien as your man, then you're together and big–and you get it right, your brain is right, and you see things, hey?

So, to be part of the team that shapes it, its gotta be the Doctor. And the deal is sweet– see he works on me–like my personal coach, finding the something-more, the getting to be what I am.

. . . and those guys, the DDDN thumpers, they drift in, drift out. Adrenalin rising, but no day-by-day with me. Hey! I got potential–and if the stronger one brings me in, I'm in.

He shapes my world, day by day. Maybe the fighting stops–if he wants it, he's got it– that's my oath.

Chapter 122
ALLA-WUZ MEETS AN OLD FRIEND

Amah standing before me: he looks somewhat embarrassed, more after eyeing my trunk than me.

"I need you to be in the classroom after school tomorrow."

I find weak voicing available.

"Oh, why?"

"It's a secret," and a half-smile, such as when he gave a present on my third birthday or when we together had played one side and had won well at lunchtime games in Grade 1.

"Oh…" and barriers in the brain made it difficult to talk more. Small chit-chat was something reserved for friends.

And suddenly I remember who he is, find voice. "I'll be there, yes, because we were friends once."

"Once?" and the startled look in his eyes. How often after that look would he have turned to his best bud for help. But that was long ago.

"Yes, once. You haven't been around for a long time."

"I've been… I've been…" A pause, a slight shuffle on his feet from side to side, as though remembering volumes, experiences which had come so densely they took time just to remember. "Things have happened," and he squinted at me in half-hope, half-plea.

"Yeah, but friends don't just walk away. Friends help, friends aid:- you in your stuff, I in mine. But look, that's old. I'll be there, because you used to be my friend. Bye," and I push past a gawping shoulder, past a troubled eye which had been too blind too long.

Chapter 123
MEETING

I glanced around the corner of the classroom. They were both there–Alla-wuz and Tahla, looking both somewhat angry. I realized I was late.

"Hello! I'm here."

Stony silence.

"I asked you to come because I've got something exciting–or someone exciting–to show you."

Silence again.

"Presenting a 'new' friend!" Leaning back towards the door, I called, "Come on in."

Jort strode in like a steamroller smoothing roads.

Uproar . . . Alla-wuz jumped to his feet, "Him! Are you mad?"

Tahla: "Yahoo with him now?"

Alla-wuz: "You got us here so you and he could beat us up."

I: "No, it's all right. He's with us now."

The stability was somewhat less than wet ice.

"He's with the Doctor too."

"I don't believe it."

"No, really. . ." I hadn't' expected the meeting would go like this–Alla-wuz like a decaying throbbing tooth, and Tahla stabbing thorns.

"No. He's got the right of it. The Doctor shapes my world."

A snigger like thorns.

But only one of the tooth and thorns was unsure. "So you don't fight the Foctor's dollowers?"

"No, in truth."

"People say you go with the night gangs and raid the followers, beat them up.

"Once I did. But the past has left."

"And if it gets you into trouble with the night gangs?"

"It's done–on my oath."

"But why–nigh wow?"

"Perhaps I can elucidate," and a gray-headed creature entered the room.

Tahla smiled widely "How cute–where's its control?"

Alla-wuz was more acerbic. "This is one of your flying snakes?"

"Backhanded in art, son. Allow me to pour out offerings on the waters." He looked at our expressions. ". . .to tell you something of me. "Let me prove I am a fellow servant of the Doctor and see scenic more than you. Tahla, your next document you are working on includes the line, "Blessed are they who cremate mince the same," And Alla-wuz, at three o'clock in the morning, you wrote poetry. One could say," he said dryly, "that you de-elucidated poetry."

Twenty teeth made a rapid downward movement, hanging vacantly in space as mouth muscles unexpectedly relaxed in surprised shock.

"I, er, I..."

"How nood you co that? Actually its "Blessed are those who create peace; the same men shall be blessed."–the other is just silly . . . But how, how could you know? I heaver nab written any ping to thayper.

And Alla-wuz: "I was all alone. No one was there. How..."

Silence sat as queen over several seconds.

"I have arrived from your future. Your past is easily read, your future too. For instance an automobile will unnecessarily cause engine over-action in five seconds from ... now."

Three puzzled half-smiles.

On time, a car revved loudly around the street corner near the school.

Jort: "See how he shapes you."

General silence for five seconds, then a hubbub of excited acceptance.

I relaxed, letting tension seep into some distant drain–it was going to be alright.

"But why here? Why now?"

"Your group was about to fracture."

"So?"

"Your future is prehistoric and key to us."

"What? How?"

"Your future is important to us."

"But..."

"Your social and emotional interpersonal connectives need to stay resilient and adaptable to provide maximal positive future impact."

"Oh?"

"You are important to us . . . You are also always important to the Doctor. I am authorised to show you my small-scale timecraft."

"Darpin?"

The grey smiled. "My timecraft. It allows me to travel between times..."

"Oh."

Almost as an afterthought, he added, "...and anywhere in the Universe."

I was excited, "Nifty!"

"urIf you like, we can visit my time-space slate, visit my planet. Would the proposal be agreeable and facilitative to you?"

A furore of excitement. And of acceptance.

"We can go now."

Alla-wuz pointed out the flaw in the plan: "Our parents are expecting us very soon— we've already been here fifteen minutes."

Afra smiled. "My friend, reframe your logical inconsistency. Recognise that, given current data, that if one were given a timecraft, one could leave now, stay away two days, and return to a time one minute after initial departure time."

Tahler had decided. "Get's low!

And the corner was turned. Down the stairs, out between two buildings to empty space, to a ship that suddenly appeared as we approached.

The entry, the sealing, the hum

Chapter 124
WORLDS IN A CLICK

As Afra opened the door, we were face-to-face with a rippling sunset. Reds and oranges interleaved and rippled greens and blacks gently aside in falling waves of light. Two half moon crescents lay lazily on their side, enjoying the show. The tall-stalked trees sighed as a wind rippled by.

"Now, to maximise Lattice structures and inputs to adjust peripheral configurations, I am requesting you interact with the . . . the computer I would think you would call it—as a first step, tell it your nomenclature. It will be able to give you informational notes as you move around this world, and will continue to facilitate thusly as long as you are here."

He paused for a moment, then continued, "The computer has informed me based on reviewing how I interacted with you earlier that my words may have been a little difficult to understand. So we'll try again, OK. It is not necessary, but it will greatly help if you tell the computer who you are. It will always be your guide as you move around this world."

We agreed, and a small bead was placed on our head. The grey spoke strangely, and it glowed and snuggled closer to our skin. The next, my vision blanked out, and I could only see a vision of me. A nameless query seem to drift across my head—something like "identify:" or "name:" or "caption:" I spoke my name, and was startled to hear three other voices murmur, "Alla-wuz", "Tahla", "Jort".

An impression of stillness as a verb somehow formed in my head, and then my body seemed to freeze solid. An image of a digital clock swam into my vision. It started at 10:00:00 and commenced a count down. Ten minutes became nine, then eight. Finally my limbs relaxed again, followed by a quick warm flush of pleasure. Full-formed words seemed to enter my ears.

"Welcome to the Living Lattice Portal. Since you are entering for the first time, I would like to assure you that our ten trillion inputs/second, including from your world in both your hometime and in related time-linked data are devoted to improving the quality of service. Standard operation mode of read/write to organic tissue is set, together with maximum privacy setting from other lattice users. This can be varied anytime, specially with close friends, such as data suggests your group to be."

Slight pause.

It proceeded:- "Exit from any on-line experience is via triple tongue click, such as can be made by lightly touching, then removing the tongue to and from the top of the mouth. This enters a wait state, so you can choose to edit settings or data. A further triple-click removes you from the system. A further triple-click at any time will return you to the portal.

"Triple-clicking at that point will cause an extrusion into your near realspace of a representation of a call centre staff member, who will personally assist you with any queries.

"Continual triple-clicking will be understood as a call to efficacious aid in personal emergencies, and an emergency relief worker will immediately be extruded to evaluate any emergency assistance you need."

I blinked rapidly.

The voice paused, then, "It is understood that you have exhibited a motion consistent with bewilderment in your species. Triple-click your tongue if you require assistance."

After some seconds of silence, it continued. "So triple-click exits current function. Repeated triple-clicking brings various levels of aid. Now displaying standard interface," and round the edges of my vision suddenly appeared twelve icons with words below them.

The temptation was too much. I chose the dreamshare icon. A small figure appeared and curtsied, "By your leave, sir, I'll just access data required for maximum viewing relevance and enjoyment." I seemed to feel pages turning and fluttering in my head. Then a voice, "This product seems incompatible with your (or your species') physical and/or psychological profile. Please choose again."

Nothing delaying, I did. Again, the flicking of pages in my brain. Two seconds waiting, then suddenly I was swimming in sound. Liquid love swirled around my head, my spine, and out through the tops of my toes. Joy swam as a dolphin beside me, and on the other side a dark fish darted in and away, in and away. The sun danced and multiplied itself so one lamp of warmth and affection became two, became four ... eight ... sixteen, and all of them danced as I plunged, swooped and dove in my ocean. Somehow I knew it stretched to eternity, and I had time to reach its farthest bounds, to explore its corners, to discover fish, sunken cities of old-world hopes and dreams, and to coruscate with every being I met on my journeys. I swooped down through the velvet liquid. Then up, up and up, and I broke the surface, and suddenly I was every dolphin in the oceans, every whale in glittering seas who had ever broken their world's glistening edge and touched an alien world, felt alien air tingle pores, and seen sights and sounds and beings for their children to marvel at.

Then down. Back into velvet, and on and on as supple muscles caressed the water and turned it to their will. A shout left my throat and I knew that that was the first shout ever in all space and time to fully express the joy, the wonder, the hope of new mornings, of new loves and discovered talents. On and on, and the black fish darted in, darted in and away. All the time the sound poured on and on, a caressing love in each note. I exulted, turned, rolled, roared. Beauty as mine–I wore it like a robe and sceptre.

The dark fish darted in and away, in and away. Suddenly ahead of me, it darted toward me. Somehow my mouth opened, and it was inside. A sour taste, then suddenly a toothache, then an aching of all my body. Sorrow grew, roamed my body, roared, took control. Every nerve in my body smouldered, lit as fire, roared, flared, opened the bounds of torment, and blackness poured through me, screaming as aching need, screeching as nails through infant feet, shrieking as agony fought agony in every body nerve and shredded nerves in their aching. Music note fought against cacophony then joined in discord and fire, torment. Torture played.

And faded, leaving a sole echoing note hovering as a cry from an open mouth I realised must be mine. Suddenly the sun was there, the dark fish dead at my side, and the music played. Bass notes rolled love through my being, touching tortured nerves, leaving warmth and love.

Beauty touched again a gasping soul, and love was there, love was in each atom, love warmed, touched, held each fiber of my being.

And I was back at the Portal, a sign flashed up in my view. "Music Clip ended. Replay or return to main menu." I gasped, clicked main menu, and the icons bobbed around my vision's periphery. I slid my tongue by accident, and noticed the icons wink so they were dimmed and I could again see the real world real around me.

"What was that?" I whispered to the grey beside me.

He frowned, clicked his tongue, paused a while, then smiled. "That was a full-sense music clip."

"It was . . . beautiful."

"Yes, that one has been a favourite of many for a a few years–each ones sees it differently of course, depending on what the Lattice selects from their mind."

"What is this–this Lattice? And these pictures in my head?"

"It's our . . . computer, you might say. Everyone has access–everyone who holds the Doctor dear."

"Oh."

"With it you can . . . watch TV. You can communicate with others without words–just thoughts. You can pour a representation of your emotions into them so they understand your feelings as well, understand your world view, your depth of feeling on a subject. Millions can participate in discussions about the future, about the past, about possible action and reaction–the lattice listens to each one, and chooses which thoughts are important enough to present to the participants."

"So . . . big."

"And with it we plot the effect of altering the past, to predict how the future may change. And so we move worlds between alternities safely. But did you notice the very bottom left icon–let me show you. . ."

And then it got really interesting. . .

Chapter 125
LOSTNESS (MRS FALPUB SPEAKS)

"I hate and despise you," she said, pushing words into the brittle air. "You promise joy and I forever have pain," and she could almost hear the crack of brittle glass. Heavy words poured from a heart brittle, stretched with tension tighter than a drum.

"You came to give joy, and I have a poison well. I look inside me to draw out love and caring and warmth, and all that I find is bile, gall, and a fresh burning.

"You, Doctor, you know squat of pain. I have followed cautiously, not the big steps, followed you in the shadows, scarcely believing that one could be so big as you–and now I find you a little . . . thing, perhaps no bigger than my imagination. Your promises . . ." and she scrunched Tahla's letters, and then there was sobbing.

Chapter 126
JOURNAL OF P ULYSSES PLUGRATH III–
ENTRY 140

When I batter at you
I batter my soul

When I mow you down,
You who could have been my mother,
Do I have the right to be comforted by another?

When I club down a small boy
So he's broken, fractured, mauled,
Do I have the right to procreate one more?
When I mat your short head
With blood and exuberant gore,
Do I ever have the right
To fondly remember my father at the door?
Now judges on your lofty heights,
You cannot judge me I say!
For how can you possibly know
The pressures of these days?

But hush. They're at the door. We move again.

Chapter 127
TINCTURES

We walked on through the sunset and alien world. Presently, I asked, "Why doesn't the sun set?"

"What do you mean?" queried Afra.

"The reds, oranges, and greens . . . they're as strong as they were when we landed. It should be night now."

Afra smiled. "It's no sunset, Amah, it's night already. These are nebulae hanging in our sky, rippling, glowing. One fades, yet another comes, for no reason other than nature's accidents. Our race grew up with this beauty. Clothiers were amazed, scientists in awe, interior designers puzzling over its fine tinctures. We invented space travel so early, because all in our race were inspired—clothiers, interior designers, scientists, everyone—all wanted to reach those lights . . .

". . . the telescope was invented before interior plumbing."

"Oh." And indeed the colours tinted the houses near me with such delicate hues as I had never seen. And houses there were. In love with the nebulae, they sprawled like tinctured omelettes, or soared like broken waves pushing up against gravity. Holes gaped in the middle of walls passing through neatly to the other side, imitating the dark point just now sitting above it—divine painter and the created's emulation striving to touch.

And always, always, the trees spiralled.

Chapter 128
PRECIOUS
(A FRIEND OF AMAH'S FAMILY SUFFERS)

They had come through the door, mowing it down, blades hungering, seeking, accomplishing. Their last act had been to cut the phone line. He had to admire that–his day job was always about seeking efficiency, and these had had it.

And they at him...

He paused as stabbing pains coursed through left lung, right lung. *So this is what it is like to have broken ribs* wandered across his mind in search of a place to belong. Finding none, it collapsed to one knee.

Kneeling untidily on the floor, he noticed the cobwebs under the sink. *Next time* he thought. And *my thoughts are a bit muzzy.*

Why the lightness in my feet he thought *that they can't grip the ground to stand?*

Inside Aider was busy, and comfort came, a certainty of holding by another. *I can't hold the side of the table* he thought and *was that a little blood under him* was a query which sought attention.

A resting on the ground, a time to lay down.

Pain swells like thunder seeking my soul to terrify jagged across his mind, but he recalled the Son's death and knew there was love. *Relationships hold on* he marvelled, and *time to rest the hand beside me. In the air's too high.*

Aider recalled to him that precious to the Doctor is the death of his faithful believers, and he marvelled at the poetry and life that seemed now to flow from these words.

He remembered the uncertain man with the baseball bat. He had looked into the rapidly blinking eyes and thought *this man would be nervous at a librarians' convention* and then he . . . and then the pain came.

It comes again, and gasping was an autonomic reaction. *I can't feel my back against the floor. Shouldn't I?* and pain found his right side and shook it like walls hitting the head on one side *like hitting a car* he wondered and *my thoughts are muzzy. Clear thoughts. I love clear thoughts* found passage to his head through the pain and *its big now how big can pain get.*

Autonomic need–deep gasping, a groan. How strange. *The body breaks. The spirit sustains* he thinks and *there is such a*

Chapter 129
SCHEDULED TEAM

"It's going well. The Mayor is pleased."

"The teams *are* working well."

"One thing though. The boy we recruited to take photos on the night: the word is, he's turned. He wasn't on last night's trip, and he was seen with Doctor-ites."

"Oh… Make an example of him and of the family. Zero tolerance is best at the start of this sort of thing. Keep everyone in line."

"When?"

"Where are we up to in the diary?"

Pause.

"All drawn up until a week from tomorrow."

"Pencil him in for then. And the family. Not much left, if you know what I mean."

Chapter 130
OPEN HOUSE

"I finally got her to sleep." A sigh. "She's a mess. Coming home from nightshift, seeing her husband like that. And no phone line. She had to stagger down half the street before finally finding someone to answer the door."

"Hmm…"

"Thanks for not going to work today, honey. I just couldn't have … not without your help–getting her things, and …"

"It's alright."

"Where's it going to end? Such nice people they were, just … just like you and me without the kids."

"Speaking of kids, will they be alright–it's like our night all over again."

"But what can we do? We can't have her out in the street."

"Yeah … when's Amah due home?"

"Any time now."

Chapter 131
THE BETTER WIDGET

I looked about at the scene beyond the doors of the room. The timecraft reflected the nebula hovering behind it. "You world looks cool."

He smiled. "It's a pleasant alternity. It soars in catalogues–it seems to be working out well."

"Pardon?"

"Alternity number 6127531 seems pleasant. Revision dated 10 days ago by your reckoning."

"Pardon?"

He frowned, "Listen a little, boy. This is the 6127531st revision from the founding of our republic."

"Oh."

"Another change is being debated tonight on the Lattice."

There were sounds beside me as Alla-wuz and Jort returned to reality, and so it all had to be explained to them. The grey frowned at Tahla, who was still oblivious to us, then he clicked and stared into space. Ten seconds later, they were both back.

"It's amazing," he blinked at us. "Their library... And I bound a fook I borrowed from our town library last year which had had the last part ipped rout, and I was table ooh...

Afra interrupted. "Come children. See my world."

Chapter 132
VALOUR

I couldn't sleep, so I got up to watch the sky ripple.

But green splashes were exciting for only so long, so I choose games from the Lattice array–it had been recommended in swirling colours, so I entered.

"*Advance, player, and be recognised!*"

I walked toward him, my feet echoing on cold black marble. The walls swirled, marble imitating nebulae.

"*Ah, it's you, my old friend. How's the old mallethand?*"

I looked–and my hand was indeed malleted. I swished it in the air–it felt good, it felt heavy, it felt lethal.

I smiled, "How are you, old friend?" clasping his shoulder with my other hand–muscled, bronzed.

"*I–this is nifty!*"

He bowed. "And now, honoured friend, as we move to the impending conflict, allow me to travel with you until the strife is joined, till perhaps the battle separates us, each to his own destiny, each to his own reward."

"*OK . . .*"

"*And shall we travel with others, the camaraderie of a large band of like-minded souls, or perhaps just you and I, learning new skills together, and for the telling of deeds of renown over the embers of a dying fire What shall it be, my friend?" and he hit me on the arm in a friendly manner, and the Lattice flowed into my brain the sense of a battle-hardened warrior who yet looked at me as an equal, a s a man of might, of integrity, of renown.*

And in gladness of heart, I said, "Together let us roam, together tell and forge such deeds as stir the soul, that heighten our minds' eye, that provoke us to bend the stars from their course, to turn the knave from his errand and the evil one from his prey."

"*Indeed, with delight! And now, old friend, the swarm extrudes from the higher dimension, extrudes into bodies made for them by the traitorous Hirmwhet, once so trusted and esteemed in the highest councils of the land. They extrude, fight, have their body ripped away, and yet dare to return in a fresh body on another day.*

"*Still, old friend, they forge time for such glorious deeds, such touching and shaping of time past, of valour present, and of, and for, future glories. Come!*

"*We must needs pass over the mountain pass separating the two valleys." So up and up we strode. The company being good, the day passed quickly. And then fell the night.*

We arose in the morning as ice clinked and dripped in the trees, somewhat short on temper and even shorter on sleep. But still, the chill soon fled before the morning sun, and we soon reached the crest, and looked on the fertile valley below. The villagers as ants bustled busily, and we again were soon telling tales of honour earnt by distant friends on alien shores. (The Lattice promoted (within my emotional framework) joy of bravery and striving for honour simultaneously, diminishing my uncertainty within this opening scene.)

Floating slightly askew to the ground and to my right, I noticed a thin glow rippling mid-air. The thinness solidified swiftly, until resembling a man-shaped bottle—and still it glowed.

Beside it another thin glow rippled.

"Gedathel, behold!"

"Still! It is the extrudants." Swift as thought, he drew his great sword and sliced through the three shining ripples. They punctured like worn waterskins, and a loathsome evil-smelling fluid oozed to the ground—then was absorbed into it with a prolonged hiss.

"The extrudants have found us, old friend. The battle is soon here." He swept his keen sight across the peaceful pastoral scene, then pointed in the direction of our so-recent ascent. There a score of bottles glowed green under the shadows of the trees. And over to our right they also festooned, numbers such as fill a warrior's heart with joy and yet foreboding.

Then as a bottle filling up with liquid colour, with shape, a living being poured into each simultaneously, and they were upon us. And yet, beyond their shoulders, more green ripples danced.

And we turned, Gedathel and I, to the battle, our backs together, he with two glittering great swords such as only he could wield, and I, mallet-handed and with a crossbow that was always primed. We strove together in the bucolic land, strove in bitterness of spirit against those who would take our lands, our wives, all hope, would take all lives.

The roar of the horde, the roar of Gedathel, he of the two swords, and the rapid twang twang of the crossbow, the cry of the fallen enemy (their green falling into the grass), the smell like a myriad crushed roaches at the passing of each, the wielding of the mallet for those who would circle from the side, the sweat of Gedathel's back against mine, the shifting of feet, the striking down of the enemies, the thrusting and withdrawing of the great swords from fractured green sides, the fatigue that fevered at the corners of our eyes, that tugged unbidden at muscles that must needs discharge their duty, the stinging of sweat in our eyes, the holding, the faithful keeping of each our watches.

Gedathel and I laboured completing our charge, our appointed call. Then the rippling of green in the air, the pouring forth of an extrusion of Hirmwhet (the traitor, the great enemy). The traitor's smirk as he turned, as he turned with a great sword spinning nimbly in a doubly-jointed wrist, and the roaring of Gedathel as he saw the traitor and rushed forward, forsaking me, and the stumbling down of Gedathel from a extrudant knave's blow to his exposed back, and then the fall and the fall and the

And Gedathel lay prone, the knave over him raising a sword, razor sharp, a sword never before having felt the cutting of human flesh. And the raising, the base savage joy of the knave, the nameless pit in my stomach.

And I turning, turning to aim my bow...

But lo! The battle call, the charge from the trees of a new face, the striking of the extrudant as he hesitated between the fallen quarry and the new threat.

And with a roar, my crossbow rising. Crossbow moving... and the arrow away.

And the villain fell, splashing green over Gedathel. The new figure reached Gedathel, raised him to his feet with one hand, whilst with practiced skill cutting away the life from two of the enemy.

Then the forming of we three back to back as a triangle of life, fending against the fallen green things which kept coming.

Or so we thought, for at the swelling of our numbers, they lost heart quickly and disappeared into green ripples, leaving we three on a green-drenched hillside beneath a sun daring to peek, to touch, to warm the hearts both of warriors and of those whom they protect.

Then presently, crossbow dropped, great swords yielded to gravity, the adrenalin faded to bone-heaviness, and we turned to the sudden rescuer, who even now removed his battle helmet. And the word "Father" tore from Gedathel's throat.

They embraced, father and son, re-united. And Gedathel cried before the listening heavens. "Truly today you are more than my father. For once you gave life to me—and today you have given life again. More than a father—indeed a father from heaven you have become."

And they embraced with tears.

Chapter 133
DAY OUT

Up, up. Beckoned by the alarm clock, Falpub rose in haze–sleep lay around her, a sea of miasmic calmness around her body, a haze of irreality around every thought. Thankfully habit steered her as harbourmaster through the complex rocks of the morning routine. Her, then mother, then a little more for her, and then mother again.

Irritation growled, hid itself in glass houses, snapped at Mum. The slight twitch in a hand, the black mood plotting to be heard. "No, No," she pleaded. "Not the long dark slide into gloom, into depression . . ."

So flee for the moment, mentally trace the long ferry ride down her favourite childhood river in the ferry, waves chopping, birds and breadcrumbs at ferry stops. The untouched mysteries in the nearest unexplored field, township, mysterious cave, unbounded air balloon.

Presently a little better. But only a little....

Today! she declared, today would be hers! She would pour love into herself, would pretty up her interior with music, pour attention and rightness into herself and her hair, seek the soothing of succour, invest the indigent (herself) with indulgence and just a little insolence!

So, into the world, into the hairdressers, into the café, into the aromatic soap store, into the cup of rich foam that sat all defenceless on the table before her, into the beautiful beautiful cake that promised to be her friend and sit beside (or under) her for the next five years, into the sun and the long leisurely walk down shady treelines to home...

And so she turned from the treeline into the last street. Last one before hers drifted across her mind. But a dog turns at the bottom of the street while she walks down, walks down. Yet she walks on, walks on, waiting for it to go, to flee into its yard, walks on– then slowly suddenly in slow motion realise it will not move.

And she turns, unsure, and returns up the hill.

Finally she pauses near the street corner, trembles–then turns and retraces the treeline and sun back to the last café–and sits . . .

and sits and presently another rich foam drink.

A rising, a taxi, a detailed set of streets–a route that avoids very carefully, even by taxi, that painful lurking corner.

Chapter 134
JOURNAL OF P ULYSSES PLUGRATH III– ENTRY 142

O for the heart of a child with its sense of justice–it dares call something wrong and boldly walks away. Home and justice and light, at this stage, are still undeniable rights. When a child, one sees Autumn leaves falling, and a sudden gust of wind comes–and they hover for a moment as birds above the ground.

When a child, there lurks no shadow of regret, of times past: opportunities are tasted with a wondering tongue. These days the new taste dissolves on the tongue into bitterness and just the sense of a missed chance.

Now there are only regrets, and a road chosen that brooks no interruption, no slowdowns, now exists–just a road with the speed creeping ever upwards.

The child has walked away. And I am held, imprisoned with not enough innards to walk me away

Chapter 135
HERITAGE

We stood there on that battlefield, the fallen all around us, at reunion of father and son. They embraced as though the world depended on the embrace. Presently Gedathel broke from the holding and cried, "And what of my mother? What news of my sister?"

"Your sister rides forth to war too, she and her band of female warriors. She was so weighted down with sharpnesses–arrows and the like–as to make any attempt at embracing painful. Hah!" and he smote Gedathel on the shoulder with a force which might well have felled trees. "And she who bore you is well. She reminded me of my promises made long ago. 'Promise me,' she had said when I had given seed for you, 'that this little one–be it man or woman at its growing–will have all strivings, all workings of such strong hands as yours to rush its full potential on–as warrior, poet, or worker here on our farm, our home.' And she kissed me again then at that time, at the seed giving." A sudden roar, "Don't flinch, boy. Embarrassment isn't for the battle warrior. Meet my eye…

"Now, I promised her. And in such perilous days as these, I have left the farm–briefly– to seek your soul's health and growing.

"Oh, and she bade me tell you this," and he recited something learnt by heart.

166

"'How can one ever be alone? If it were only one and the Maker versus a protagonist, versus the Traitor, versus all of the extrudants as one, it is as if you and a power higher than all the accumulated suns are versus 1 or 10 or 100 fleas."

He stopped, and gave a proud lop-sided grin. "There, that's her saying. She bid me memorise it . . . and I did. And you know your mother, boy. In matters of maternal devotion and its outworkings, she is not to be thwarted. And your aunt–she of the seven cows–has found a husband. It has been said that on a dim morning, there is not much difference to the casual eye between the husband and the cows... But she is indeed well, and the progeny– ugly or not–wished strength and vigour and easy birth... "Oh, and your second cousin, Tiewth, has fallen to the extrudants. He fell fighting with full strength, all alertness, and is with the Maker. He sees Him, as we all will one day. The Maker's dwelling is not with human flesh, but we who believe are bidden to his house on our ceasing here. and he is there..."

"I know of a land, a world," I said, "where the Maker came to help out a sickness, was felled by the creators of the sickness, and overcame even that to vanquish the plague. And now he lives in the hearts of his warriors."

He sniffed. "Such a tale is not for me. Maybe in each world, the Maker works differently. But this sounds only fancy tales to distract from the deeds before us.

And our neighbouring lands–news has reached us–are reeling before the fell creatures too. Struggling rightly–but struggling–in times as these, son, in times as these..." and he stared sombrely at the peaceful rural scene spread out below us in the valley. "...Maker willing, may each of us live to reach the full potential wrapped up, buried in each double helix of life."

Chapter 136
CHORES

Mum came back from calming the new guest.

"I've given her some brandy, and she's fallen asleep. Where is Amah?'

Father looked up from the verandah, sanding paper in hand.

"You know it's still early. He'll be home in a hour. Must have mis-read the clock."

"When will you lop those trees?"

"Try for this evening, hey?"

"That's when you were going to fix the clothesline."

"Oh . . . I'm in the middle of something, dear."

"That's the way it is. I'm too busy... I'm busy... I'm ..."

Pause

A small voice. "Sorry."

A holding.

"As soon as we can, let's go. Another place. Please!"

"Go?'

"Move. I hate this . . . city. I hate this street, this patio you're always working on."

A little tension in the voice: "It's necessary to take the time to get this right The sun shines brightly there in the afternoon, and any visitor at that time can clearly see any imperfections."

"Oh!" A little disgust. "OK!"

"And shortly we lop trees. There's time."

"Fine."

"I've got to keep going, if we're to get everything done, OK?"

"OK. Watch the time."

"Sure. We'll get it done in time." Not meeting the eyes.

A bending to work. A harder re-evaluating from the one standing, as though something had happened which troubled her.

From inside, a drunken snore drifted down the hallway.

Chapter 137
ORTHINOR

We travelled until there was large-grained sand in our shoes and larger grained sand in our eyes. Fatigue lurked in our muscles and sabotaged all effort to speak. Still it was still enough to pull together, to share our cause, our fight, our transparency before the Maker.

One came leaping down the hillside, his song echoing from rock fell to granite block. We watched him through eyes filled with grit and with a weariness that washed a world grey and tasteless. The Lattice caused every bone to ache–and held back exhaustion within a hairsbreadth.

And so he came on us as effervescence into water, as the tingling of the fingers when gladness arrives.

"Hold, good companions," he cried. And on reaching us, "Hail! I am Orthinor of the Valley of Sands beyond the Swamp of Drifting Trees. And he approached each, one by one. "And you my good sir?" to Gedathel's father...

"Yrelteral," roared he. "And a warm greeting to you, my friend. Tell us of your family and of your times."

"Sir, I am beholden to the noble Sir Trinstalsa there, for it is he who has noticed my humble beginnings, and has raised me almost as son. He has sent me forth to live his heart for adventure, and to promote his call to embrace the Hidden Makers."

"The Hidden Makers? Whatever do you mean? There is only one Maker, the maker of all, who is over all and in all. Why then 'Hidden Makers'?"

"Why , I mean that our path to the full exaltation of the next life is through a series of hidden things to be discovered–through a series of revealings to be experienced each supervised by a particular new Maker. The Maker we knew is only the first of so many many more glorious Ones."

"How do you say this? What is your authority?"

"Why, by vision. I have never believed in the Maker–but one night I dreamed of a ladder, each with a different Maker. That is how I know 'tis true."

"And we stand here as former strangers–and now companions well-met!" And on we travelled together–for strangers met in a strange land long delay their partings. And the day, like us, wearied...

Chapter 138
STORIES AT THE INN

Sometime later, the evening stars warred the day, blazed and spiralled, comets and fallings, bringing in the slippery night, easing it past the rampants and strivings of day, pushing back the lightness of sky. The lattice flooded me with deep weariness, of bones fatigued, and not a little hunger. Yonder, under the soaring cliff nestled a village and inn, and we strode on, somehow more vigorous, past farm and fell, past sleepy houses with matriarchs lifting the window curtain and peering out (vainly waving their raised candle). Past the dust settling on the roadside after the busy busy day, past the shadow of passers-by rising towards us in the failed sunlight, past the town signpost, past the town elder rising from the judges' seat, helped homeward by his strong wooden staff and a grandson's even stronger shoulder. The glinting of the falling falling sun on the newly washed shop window, a spark of life reflected in our own eyes. Civilization, our cradle, our respite, and in time our bewhiskered beings' evening seat. And past little children already wearing their night gown and chased by their mothers inside.

The inn seeped its aromas past its heavy closed door—upon opening, it poured out its smells and heart into us—vegetables, warmth and music that beat against our body like a lost child beating on a new drum. E'en the cold shadows on the wall knew that warmth would soon come to these rooms.

And gladly we entered.

The musicians sat at their instruments, in love with their craft. Their listeners entered the inn in love with melancholy, with the soaring anxious melody that poured forth from the world outside, from the harsh bass thrum of the spiked anger of the work and frustration that rules a person's day... But the musicians with melody and gentleness ruled bravely against the listeners' fear and fury—and as they played, each frustration slowly unpeeled itself from listeners' souls, humbly went and squatted quietly at the door like so many shoes waiting for their owners as they left. Cymbals shimmered, the lutes sang, the singers crooned and soothed. Soothed as did, indeed, the seats into which we slid, the very last in the crowded room, crouched half-hidden at the back of the room. Trees or giants seemed to inhabit the table at our side, drinking clouds and spice from upturned caves of tankards.

A being of frills and cascading curls shimmered a moving pert nose, beautiful lips and wafting perfume as she passed. Just then, the musicians launched into a song dear to her heart, and she, even while standing there, briefly sang her soul, a soaring counterpart of the musicians' plaint—her treble descant glimmered down, hugging her curls, turning back time, relieving a sorrow. And our hearts too, at her song, fled petty concerns, searched—and somehow, in this song, our hearts found and were found. There was a rebirth again of love, of hope, of rightness and realness, of the call and echo of love. Then overflowing tankards of the frothy spice all around, the starting of a new song, the lady leaving and resuming her waitressing. A raising of tankards, a deep deep drinking–and the menthols and sugars purged into the tired corners of my being, lifting, re-vitalizing, promising. Even the shadows on the wall began to warm up. And with a rousing shout from our table and the deep deep rumble from the table next us, we joined the song.

Seven shanties and three lovesongs later, we rested our tired voices and immediately ordered large meals, Long long nights on the mountain passes had surely earned such repast, and they soon arrived, steaming and fit to overflow. Payment was demanded, and I fumbled about my person. I found strange items in one deep pocket, and Lattice told me two would be adequate for the meals.

And greens and oranges, reds and browns were ingested with vigour. Presently we looked around, sated.

An earnest cleric stood up to lead a sing-song in parts. After a tremulous clearing of the throat, he commenced to sing a more serious refrain, and we as echo:-

He: Leads to nonsense.

We: Nonsense, nonsense! Leads to nonsense? no-o-o-o-no-no-no-nonsense!

He: Seeking the statistics–what?

We: Nonsense, nonsense! Leads to nonsense? no-o-o-o-no-no-no-nonsense!

He: Process of seeking the statistics–what?

We: nonsense, nonsense! Leads to nonsense? no-o-o-o-no-no-no-nonsense!

He: Oh! The juxtaposition of factual data and an arbitrary set of boxes into which the statistics must fit–whoah! What?

We: nonsense, nonsense! Leads to nonsense? no-o-o-o-no-no-no-nonsense!

He: Now in parts! This half first!

And off we sailed into parts, then into double-speed parts, into a strange combination of one-half fast and the other half of the voices double-slow, then finally fast for the first part and double-slow for the "leads to nonsense" swirling rhythm with alternate words missed. The shadows on the wall fell about with merriment.

An elderly man stood up as the shadows became cosy and the room warmer with tales and tankards. There was something about the elder, a sense that here was a commander of men, a leader followed by men, and that although his eye had hollowed, had faded, had more often uncertainty in it than direction, a whiff was there, whiff enough for even the shadows to lean forward to listen.

"It is fifty years to the day, my friends, since setting sail for the southern ocean, seeking a rumoured land, and returning to rumour, innuendo and dissembling. My men and I saw

wonders, and yet they are considered by all to be fanciful spinning of lies. But today, today, you will hear again," and bitterness edged, as arsenic, his voice, and fists danced on the edges of the hollow eyes.

"We set sail, unbidden, men willing to find wonders or to stumble into death whilst trying. At first we made good time despite emerging and clinging seaboard illnesses...

"Then we came to a sea choked with herbs–aye, a sea I say–for although there was only water all around, the herbs grew so thick as to hinder, to fight, our ship's very progress. We struggled on for days before a light wind, forsaken by fish who hid under the green mat, forsaken by birds who had come to know our hungry ways.

"And then the wind stopped, fleeing as a refugee before the same cruel fate that had so recently fought against the fish and birds. And we lay stranded before a sun rejoicing in its strength, water and food dwindling. Even more desperate, each man guarded his water supply as gold–men offered gold for another's water with fervent entreaty–and the ship's cat walked in fear of its remaining lives.

"And then one day she went missing. A search for her failed... And then nature in very revulsion against the crime committed spat us out–I mean, such a torment of wind and rain came against us, and we ran. Ran before that wind for fifteen days, ran while the waves scattered green necklaces of herb around our head.

"And then we came to a land where the sun ruled. Rain sulked in corners, scurrying out briefly then away. The inhabitants were dark, and had curved sticks they threw at their prey. By some trickery–I know not how–if they missed their prey, they were able to whistle the weapon back to themselves."

Someone snickered.

"I know, I know. I could not believe it either–curved wood that knows its mind like a trained bird–but I saw it again and again.

"So did all the crew. But they deny it these days, chasing public favour over truth and honesty...

"I brought back a dead animal found in the stream there–a marvellous thing! A duck's bill, fur like a badger, and wicked hooked stings on its back legs, and I..."

It was too much. The inn laughed him to scorn and he fled before them into the night.

I latticed that maybe it was time for bed, and I sat silent amidst the calling for tankards, the crashing of tankards, and shadows on the walls that clinked cups, sang, caroused and sought the underneaths of tables.

An old woman stood, and her voice even turned the shadows to hear. "Let me tell you of a time that heaven fought alongside earth. It was a time for heroes, and of waning of heroes."

"Hey, bar-keep," yelled a voice from the shadows, "another round of drinks. This sounds like its going to be a long one."

"Yes, and it was, a long time in the making, a long trail of blood, a long period of sorrow, of struggling to keep one's wife and children safe–sometimes unsuccessfully. But the end, when it came for the invaders, came quickly.

"One of the great scholars," and here she nodded to some strangely dressed man at the front, "had become convinced that every 205 years to the day, the meteor shows rained down, cutting furrows in the air, sizzling power and menace.

"So with desperation born of the battle, we slowly retreated, drawing the invaders towards us; yet at other points we fought desperately to gain the high ground (with great loss of life and many widows' tears) until we stood–all that remained to us of our ten thousand warriors–on the ridge and spurs of a large range and an old stone-quarry at our backs. They in front of us and to our sides, swarmed as ants, exulted as peacocks, sensed violence as lions, brooded as vultures near the imminent kill.

"It was the predicted eve of the asteroid strike. We had staked our lives on the little we had left, on merely the ponderings of a student who thought he could see an astral pattern. Nought else was left to us.

"As the sun darkened behind the hills, withdrawing midst sullen swirls of cloud, we waited, not knowing whether to live like saved soldiers or die like doomed men–only the night would tell.

"And they came! Came as promised, cutting furrows in the air, racing over the air as thunder without lightning, fire that promised destruction, yet never striking, such planets buzzing crazily near our own.

"And we knew–or had hoped–for their coming, and whilst our enemy milled in confusion–we uncovered the vast machines, the trebuchets covered at our backs–giant machines, the like of which would never be seen again in our lives. They dwarfed the workers beside them.

"And with the stones from the quarry, half the trebuchets tumbled death at the enemy . . . but half aimed much too high in the air to threaten the enemy, for there was another hope, another hope only a desperate people would have.

"For half an hour, the quarry stones flew, and our enemy recovered from the surprise, regrouped and advanced under the swirling fiery skies.

"And then–at last, what we hoped for happened. a great stone tossed into the air hit one of the fiery meteors and it shattered, shattered into a thousand pieces, each as large as a man, and the fragments hurled into the enemy camp, tearing man and beast, tearing the earth, tormenting the planet.

"And after that–all the trebuchets having found their range–it was quick. Heaven rained down on our enemies, and they found the coming of heaven a grievous thing. And we too

found the trembling of the earth, the fires from the valleys below us, and the blood that ran the riven fissures terrifying.

"And yet we walked free. And we could begin our lives again. The few left were easily routed. Dispirited–never before had heaven come to fight them–they died easily.

"And so wives and children smiled again..."

She sat down amidst silence–we could not tell her truth from the weaving of embellishments.

And then a cheer for the heroes, for the weaving of a spell of words, or for the courage in telling the weaving–we knew not what, but it was worth a cheer from the stalwarts there, from the trees and giants, from the cosy shadows.

And a pause to drink again, as the waitresses ran to fill empty tankards that were being thumped on the table. The next table with its huge huge men like trees started to sing their own foreign song–one staggered up and attempted to lead us, but a fellow giant at his table pushed him back to his chair. He teetered and fell into another, so that it smashed, becoming a thousand toothpicks. "To bed," they decided, and we felt that earth itself was labouring as giants and trees moved to their rooms. At long last the room fell clear of such, and the building foundations near us eased a little. And still the owner's eyes roved–to aid, to turn the tankards from empty to sloshy overflowings, to seek tellers of songs and stories . . .

Around the warm room, some eyes had fallen silent, watching only the fire as it crackled and flamed, others talked of new-forged swords, of wieldings against extrudants, of victories, of escapes, of quelling of fears, of wildbeasts and of enemies; others of personal moments, of longings for families and friends in far-off counties and lands, of dead friends who had shone in battle and still yet shone in their hearts; others of strategies and tactics and raids to force the extrudants back. I slouched in the capacious chair, sleepy, still and warm in my own cocoon, surrounded by raucous bulls.

Some others left, helped out by friends, but the company too good, I could not bring myself to leave, felt that with Gedathel and his father, the world belonged to justice, to right, lay inextricably in law the property of light, of goodness, of righteous and valiant hands. Still, some part of me prowled alert, always on the look out for my friends, always the guard against the beast in men or even the shadows crowding the corners in their convivial laughter and tumbling under the tables, their raucousness turning a little wild.

There was a roar to one side, a sudden pounding up of an older, a younger, the older catching the younger by the ear. "Such as my flesh and blood will never be guilty of such a thing. To conspire against the widow living next you, to seize house and land of a destitute widow whose husband died a hero–this will never be said of my son!" The old man drew his blade and the shadows gasped. He swung–only the flat of the sword against his son–but so hard as to threaten bone and health. He roared, "To take of stolen goods from widows before *you pass to the Maker is thieving from the Maker—it is the same." Another swipe—and the son fled the room.*

There was a murmur around the room. We all knew the life of each individual was the life of the group; the Maker laboured for each one of his sheep, we laboured each one of us for the group. The group for the one; the one for the group.

Silhouettes slowly turned and talked of battles won or lost, of political timings, of past and future victories. Others bent over new battle gear, admiring workmanship—the shadows leant forward with interest.

I cut a small slice of bread with my own dagger, the waitresses becoming too sleepy for alertness, and Orthinor who had not fitted at our table but had sat elsewhere, stood up to speak. "Brothers, let me tell you a tale where death was faced and beaten, where barriers were broken, and the right is triumphant.

"Visualise this: a man lies dying, his wife in tears. I come, as the Fifth Maker calls me, to their side. The standard Maker is no good here—it requires a higher. I bend my knees and implore the Fifth Maker to raise him up."

"And did he?"

"There was no immediate sign of improvement. Ah, but I kept praying."

"And?"

"Death came and hovered. There was no visit by the Fifth Maker yet (I knew the common Maker would refuse. . .) And the man ceased his body." "

Then your prayers had no effect?"

"No. After he died, the prayers worked."

"Then he came back to life?"

"Wait! I called two friends, and we stood around the body and prayed for two hours to the Seventh Maker. No change. Then we prayed more fervently for an hour to the Eighth. And . . . the body warmed up!"

"It warmed?"

"Yes, it warmed! I think he was starting to come back, but decided not to. So he died, and they cried, and I was sad."

"He died?"

"Yes."

The audience turned in their chairs and conversation rose in volume, and although Orthinor tried to talk louder, none listened. At last he sat down next to us.

"But I don't understand," he said. "Didn't they see—prayer changed things. What more proof that the Maker is wrong, and my new teaching right?"

Silence reigned.

Chapter139
SLEEPY

The Lattice home screen came up on my view. I realised I was bathed in cold sweat.

The Lattice prompted, "One moment, please..." Presently I started to feel better, and staggered to a normal bed (such as I could find in Alternity 6127531).

As I drifted off to sleep, my brain replayed a momentary point in the game, feeling the tiredness carry me away...

"I pulled shut the latticed inn window, and quickly abluted. Night poured me to bed. Up up the stairs, found the room (the travel stain'd clothes in one corner, smelly and as far from the bed as possible).

"The feather pillows, the well-used blankets that yet tickled the nose, and just time for one luxuried stretch . . . "

Chapter 140
BREAKFAST

Morning brought us to the table, sleepy but vitamins and adrenalin, protein and interest sparking vigour in the new day. Jort and Tahla seemed to be clicking and sharing unpalatable breakfast combinations:- pepper people and the shaper together was all wrong–at least for gastronomy... I sat next to Alla-wuz–he seemed a little puzzled, a little distant.

Strange being after strange being flooded the large room, but curiosity had been strictly forbidden in our group before 10 am, and I kept my tired eyes down, with just an occasional hopeful comment passed to Alla-wuz. Afra sat with us, but said little, respecting the need for a slow morning awakening.

After the meal had been cleared, Afra announced, "Children, we'll go back today, I'll return here and spend some time preparing for the Alternity Revision Consideration meeting. So back into the timecraft . . . and back to a world that looked a minute older than when we had last seen it, and much much more tattered and frayed.

The large clock on the school tower showed we had been away less than 25 minutes. We all hurriedly adjusted our wrist watches, antiques that looked too novel, too whimsical. I thought there was a technosnake on the top of the tower, but I blinked, and then there was nothing to see.

Afra cleared too small, too falsettoed a throat, "Children, I will return very soon. Because the Lattice connection still exists in your brain, you will all hear me in your head.

You will know it is I because simultaneous intracranial intercommunication will . . . sorry, you will all hear me at the same time. It is likely that it will be important, and thus important to listen. Do you understand?

"Good. To each and in each and from each the Maker!"

He bowed slightly, bid "Goodbye."

Chapter 141
A PREVIOUS EPOCH

I in the door, looking like 4 pm, feeling an eternity older.

"Hello, dear," Mum greeted me. "Something sad happened this morning, and Mrs Iugal is here. She's had a bad upset, and I've put her in your bedroom for just a little while.

"But I've got something!" she continued, "Just so much fun! You can do camping in the living room–sleep on the lounge in your sleeping bag; have the torch and some of your favourite camping food. How . . ." tentatively, "how do you like it? It'll be such an adventure."

"Sure, no worries, Mum."

And I walked on, thinking of other things. I could almost feel Mum's jaw drop behind me.

Chapter 142
NEXT DAY

We rose, we three, the next morning, to task of re-stocking our food. Soon enough complete, we set off once again toward the battle.

A beggar crouched near the city gate, and we pressed alms into his hand, "The Maker be with you." He as I as one in the Maker's hand.

And above us, the last of the night clouds rolled themselves to other climes, other callings. The sun hastened to execute its plan of a glowing arc of possession across its territory for yet another day. I could imagine its diurnal loop, some blazing dim disc, almost some timecraft that owned and recalled, resumed and recast each day, eternal, always to the heavens the same, and to the planet, always a weavng of new plots, new mysteries, new solutions, always a new casting asides of solutions from days before. And always above the recasting, the rescinding, the redacting, the remaking–a Maker. The sense of his giving, the thrill of his writings, the honour of his seeking, the absolution of being found.

Orthinor came to us just outside the town, and entreated us to allow him passage. We looked at his arms—they were not such as of fighting men, but we suffered him as a fellow traveller. "Bless you!" he cried, "And hold, for I will ask the Eighth Maker for a blessing upon you that you will understand new things, that you will become a deeper being, far beyond the writings of what you think is the only Maker." But Gedathel whacked him with the flat of the blade, and he was silent.

We still suffered him passage.

Chapter 143
SNAKE PLAN

Priority Message from Shipcommand to all pilots and auxiliary staff.

Grey sighted with infiltrated inhabitants. Seek to capture timeship as first priority. Prepare our Time Effect Kits immediate. Use of all functions authorised to procure enemy target.

Carnage in town to be carried out immediate. Distraction may force their delay, and so present us an opportunity.

Suggest firebombing west edge of town (cf procedure #1783). High possibility exists timeship is there. It will not be affected, but removing surplus structures and foliage may aid its location.

This is a major asset, strongly desired by HQ, and will rapidly facilitate new conflict in currently unreachable alterntities.

Sub-plan: Turning to us the infiltrated children seen with grey may well allow use as hostages to procure timeship (Procedures #1921-1926 authorised)

Battle Encounter Plans 162C and 162D also available for implementation.

Personal from Shipcaptain: Go! May ruthless vigour pour into your body, your tech, your eyes. Go into their fear like a surfwave.

Chapter 144
FIREBOMB

...and the western edge of the city wilted as plants before a desert wind that had not been, buildings slagged and ran down valleys like lumber tumbling into swift-flowing rivers; people wilted as dandelions on thin stalks, feeling the day's heat by hugging the ground, then suddenly were not to be found.

Such was the work of a minute. Preparing the portable time effect devices took a little longer.

Tiredly, as he broke out his Time Effect Kit, 226Y marvelled. Ironic that the strategy that currently was working best on this planet was civil war, and now they were suddenly plunged into a scenario, back into an old old scenario. 226Y's memory flitted over a bitter aeons-olds civil war felt by his own race. Thoughts, memories, roamed sourly through his mind looking for amelioraton. Finding none, they settled in adrenalin glands, and he slammed the hard pack shut, almost snapping the reluctant clasp. Slowly it moved around.

Eyes were slits as he looked around, checking that all was in readiness. "Prepared for another fracas in the family war," he thought bitterly. "Symbiosis can be such a trynj."

Chapter 145
MIDDAY NIGHTDREAM

Loud screams rent the lunch time air, and she rushed in from preparing dinner to find Mrs Iugalia in tears in front of the TV.

A frantic catching at her, the feeling of the sorrow and urgency in the grip, somehow getting her to sit on the lounge, looking to see the source of the problem.

The TV reporter on, unaware of what he had caused. "The western suburbs are gone. Here I am amidst melted ruins, looking down on what used to be a thriving business centre, then looking beyond that, down into the valley..."

Mother understood–the reporter was standing on the ruins of what had been the street formerly cozening, supporting, sustaining the lives of Mrs Iugali and a husband in what used to be happiness.

–oOo–

"Just as well the boy was at school," she thought wearily. "At least he should have a normal afternoon. Thank the Doctor it was the far edge of town that was hit."

Chapter 146
GROUP

After school the next day, the four of us sat on a playground seat. It was the first time we had ever sat together–today had been School Sports Extravanganza, and the whole day had been teams competing in the glories and defeats of swimming, athletics and ball games.

Everyone had wended their way home, but we remained. The four of us just managed to fill a whole seat, and it felt good.

"This is Afra," echoed in my head.

Tahla blinked, Alla-wuz tilted his head, and Jort whispered "Shaping!"

"This is Afra. Meet you now at Lispel Street bus stop. Note there will be recent fire damage here. Repeat: now. Any time problems will be adjusted later."

Somehow, we were no longer tired.

Chapter 147
SWARM

We headed out of town to Lispel Street and Afra. I noticed a tech snake drifting behind us.

Then to our grey friend, and greetings flowed as if long-lost mateship were suddenly renewed. "Children, I will go to my craft, "announced Afra "It's in Barton's Field. Come with me, and I'll drop you back here later." It was only a short distance, so we all turned to follow, under a sky which was unempty under the sun.

Presently, another snake joined the first . . . and another, and another, until they hovered like bees swarming, striving to block out the sun.

They swooped. Falling as hail from the sky they pounded around us, bouncing, soaring high into the air again. They poured like rain all around us, though not touching us.

"No fire, no honour," called Afra. "Remember they have tried this before with you. Only this time they are visible, as a bluff. Be of good heart, through the eyes deceive."

Then one miscalculated and came soaring down on Jort's head. Bouncing at an angle, he hit his fellow missile, and the chain effect laid techno snakes prostrate on the ground for miles. Trees splintered and cracked; shrubs pulverised, cows died.

We were able to walk on unharmed.

Gradually the swarm built again as each techno snake recovered and drifted upward again. Soon they had returned to their original numbers.

"Thigh are way doing this?" queried Tahla.

"Their first priority is the timeship–it has technology built on principles they cannot even name. Their second priority is to scatter you, if by that means I am distracted and therefore the ship becomes theirs. But stick together. Don't run in front of me. Do not fall behind. Be of good heart. Rally now, produce the smoothest gold!

"Remember only these three rules:- Stick together. Don't run in front of me. Do not fall behind. Then all will be well. There is a saying, "On a million worlds, the lonely battle is faced together"–and I say that together we will prevail.

"And remember I come from the future. I have seen the future, and this outcome I can guarantee."

And starflakes began to fall. Each pinpoint of light winked into existence just below the black swarm and drifted gently down, pausing two feet above our heads. Gradually they formed a canopy of light between us and the swarm.

"And thot are wheeze?"

"These are the giants who attend on the Doctor. I surmise he has sent them to help in our plight."

"There seems to be an awful lot of them," observed Jort, as starflakes continued to form, fall and shield at an increasing rate.

"And should it not be that such a worthy one as the Doctor should have so many servants?" inquired Afra. "Come, come, keep together. Work your feet to earn your seat."

We moved more closely together, click-clacking on the stones. The starflakes were so many now, they clearly lit up each grain of dirt on the stones at our feet.

"Why so many here now?" wondered Alla-wuz.

"To each of his own, he gives grace as their day requires. He has called here for a reason. Look, look at what approaches–and yet we still have greater numbers! We split our problem into parts–the lights can hold one part. We, the other."

"OK."

And from the hill in front of us rose another swarm of blackness. Accelerating, so each seemed to form a transient sold line from the horizon to the swarm, they shimmered, then dived as one into the ground about half a mile distant. Instantly the myriad of starflakes formed into a cube about us so that above our heads, to the right, fore and aft, it was as though we looked through a shimmering whirling galaxy at the outside world.

But we scarcely noticed–we stared at where the techno-snakes had disappeared into the ground. Then Tahla called, "Look!" There behind us, the swarm re-emerged upward from the ground, traced an arc,, and slammed back into the ground very near the original point. Half a second later, the loop was completed again; then a quarter second later, again . . . Faster and faster until the curved walls around us in the air, to our sides, appeared solid. We felt like we were marching down a horizontal funnel.

The starflakes suddenly flew away from us into the swirling mass, and there came rumblings and flashes from the battle–two ancient foes in bitter bitter conflict on yet another world.

After a while the novelty of the swirling mass wore off, and we put down our heads and trudged on.

We veered sharply onto a small path. The funnel veered too to match us.

Our heels clicked on the stone path, and just for a second, we sounded like tap dancers at the height of a routine. Alla-wuz and I looked at each other and laughed. "Shall we dance?", and we bowed as two dancers at the start of one of the old-time formal dances, and we laughed again, then moved on.

Just like old times for us!

But the path and hill were long, and we were tired long before the end of it. Occasionally a techno-snake would break through, but was immediately herded, compelled, driven back by starflake flaring to gianthood–at the first sight of an emergent giant, the snakes would flee (and these giants were so much more battle hardened than the giants I had seen up to now).

Still, there was energy in me enough to call to Alla-wuz, then for Alla-wuz and I to quickly deviate to look at a toy lying on the grass–I had lost one some three months ago, and this looked identical.

Alla-wuz and I looked down.

"It's mine. It's gotta to be mine."

"No, it can't be. Yours had a chip at the top."

"It did?"

"Yes, and this one doesn't. See?"

A technosnake popped vertically out of the ground between us.

We gawped. Alla-wuz's face contorted to fear; he turned; he ran. The snake saw it too, shot a hot beam, and much of Alla-wuz's torso disappeared.

He fell, as a giant's foot slammed down on the snake.

I ran, I ran for three footsteps of eternity to my best bud, eyes and heart trembling.

It wasn't good, and I scrambled for words for a fallen friend.

"Come, leave him! He'll be alright," came an order from 20 paces behind us.

Incoherence raved.

The hole in my friend was large, and yet I was bidden "walk on" as if all were well. I turned to face the grey, I turned to face the fool, I turned to face my antagonist.

I turned as one turns who is asked to move on after a friend is gored by a bull, and is bleeding, dying.

I turned as one who had almost lost someone ten days ago and had found them again—yet now he was being removed by force through tears.

I turned as one who had watched parent strike parent with rage, with hurt, with bewilderment—and had felt the echoe of such emotions within myself—with shame.

I turned, as a lion turns to roar.

I turned, and found Afra a handsbreadth away. I paused, and in that moment he pointed a narrow black device at me, and I froze.

Chapter 148
THE STAND

Legs pumped as iron, moving us up, away from village, away from the beggar, toward the war, towards duty, towards and through overgrown tangled plants, taking the most direct route to the pass, and already starting to regret the choice.

Ornithor curled up near a bush swivelling his head this way and that at it.

"What is it?"

"The shadow cast by the third and fourth look like hands!"

"So?"

"But you don't understand! Finding shadows showing hands reminds me of companion angels' hands, and that makes me stronger in my faith, and . . ." No more to say, he pulled out a grubby sketchbook, and quickly made a perfect rendition of the shadows falling from that particular bush at one hour after lunch on the second day after solstice.

Legs propelled, up and away, leaving him to catch up with us.

Presently we passed into a leafy bower which stretched all the way up the slight ravine we were in, and the sun danced through the hovering green above our heads, and fell gently here and there, delighted the grass, calling to the shrubs who arched their necks, raised their branches to feel more closely the attentions of their dearest friend. Birds turned their heads to sing then fell silent at the spectacle. Worms raced through the labyrinth of rejoicing roots while the green danced, even in places where no light should fall. The whole bower was luminous, even other-worldly.

"Hold! They are upon us," cried the father of Gedathel, and we whirled around and suddenly saw. Behind each dancing rippling bush the greener outline of a shape almost

filled. An unbuckling of our swords, a readying of mace and mallet. Today was a day of doing and telling, or doing and dying—all that mattered now was to do. Adrenalin sang in our ears, and fear lurked ready for attention.

And they fell, like green poison from ripe fruit shaken from a tree by gusts of ill-fortune and sorrow.

"Backs together. Face outwards!" yelled Gedathel and we moved to face each some corner of the compass, and at each direction we found extrudants formed, ready for battle.

They came upon us as an elephant at an ant, as great rolling swathes of hail upon the drought-weakened grass, as sledgehammers upon glass.

And yet we held, the three of us, besmirched by green gore as the aliens burst, fell and vanished. Sword fell upon mallet plunge upon the parry-and-thrust upon the bloody lunge of sweat and the desperately plunging swords into the heart (or so we guessed) of their physiology, the mallet to the exposed arm or leg to ready them for the finishing blow, the bleeding of pseudo-gone, the crunching of alien carapace, the spilling of blood from what might have passed for arteries. And green everywhere, green blood pouring as blasphemous rain upon a gasping earth, green eyes seeing as unseeing waves poured down upon us, each one unquestioning as a grain of seed waved on by the oncoming waves.

Rise and thrust, parry and lunge, the three of us ignored lactic acid that screamed in our arms, cramping muscles, holding back the pistoned movement needed so rapidy. Cut and thrust, lunge and parry, the sword incision in then out, readying for the next form.

Sweat and perspiration, the feeling of adrenalin fueling action fuelling adrenalin fuelling a desire to overspeed, overthink—and then the struggle to come back to coolness, maintain the balance; alertness and vigour midst clear thinking and a right heart, the three of us balanced as battlements midst surrounding cliff drops.

The three of us, I say, for Orthinor had fallen to his knees at the first sight of the green outlines with cries of "I'll save us by entreaty," and so we had formed a triangle round a figure that roared and begged, twitched and moved with such noises as embarrassed a people fighting their enemies, begged his angels and multiple Makers (disowning totally ours) with such fervour that he fell against my legs as two extrudants rushed towards me. Eagerness bubbled like effervescence in their eyes, so that one stumbled on a hollow in the trampled earth and fell, leaving the other off-balance and ready for an easy upper thrust.

"Stand, you fool! This is not the time," yelled I, and Orthinor stooped to examine shadows formed on the ground.

"A sign, a sign!" he exclaimed, jumping to his feet. "The strong charge wins the day," and he ran, blandishing his book of shadow drawings into the crowd of extrudants' outlines forming further down the hill.

And was cut down

And was cut down
He was cut down with blood.
He was cut down. Falling with blood. On the grass.
The extrudants paused as one, tilting back their heads and yowling, as a rejoicing cry
from an undead thing finding pleasure after long years of pain. The ululation rippled from
throats up and down the green gash in the mountain that had once held a leafy bower.
And the fight continued, rolled over us like a strangler's grip slowly achieving its aim.

Chapter 149
AS UNKNOWN AS CATS

"I've demobilized your muscles for several instants," hissed Afra. "Listen carefully. He looks dead but I've seen the future. I've lived the future. You will see him again very very soon. Trust me. Trust the Doctor. Doubt is as slippery as sneezes on a dark path."

An image of the Doctor rescuing Alla-wuz and I, even as his son was on trial for his life, the recall of the mighty giants encapsulated in a dancing spark of life, the enormous manpower (or giant power) gathered around now . . .

It was enough! I could believe . . .

We started to move, then I stumbled.

"Come! No fire, no honour."

We moved, two shards of people beneath a whirling sky.

Our heels clicked on the stone path, and just for a second, we sounded like tap dancers at the height of a routine. Alla-wuz and I looked at each other and laughed. "Shall we dance:", and we bowed as two dancers at the start of one of the old-time formal dances, and we laughed again.

We stopped and stared at the grey, who together with us, was back at the start of our journey. "What happened?" I interrogated.

Alla-wuz said, "Yeah, I think I just . . . whoah . . ." and his eyes grew wide.

"The enemy can do micro-time jumps under these swirling conditions, but they can't control whether forward or back. They were probably hoping for a jump forward, in all probability, to maximise what Alla-wuz remembers."

"You knew this was going to happen?"

"Yes, yes of course..."

"You could have told us!"

"I've tried this before. People typically bring up the three Time Travel Paradoxes, and then postulate the Caulzot catastrophe and argue its inevitability regardless of any Time Travel interventionary action."

"We wouldn't have." He blinked at us. "Sorry–of course not. But it is always true that if it is a matter of relying on technology or time travel to cure a problem, or to rely on the Doctor for his friendship during the crisis, it is always better to rely on the Doctor."

"And the forward time jump to a random alternity is treacherous," he continued.

"And now," he said, with a strange smile, "I believe the phrase I used was 'On a million worlds, the lonely battle is faced together.' Together, let's fight our battle."

And we walked again each step of our previous route, walked while the horizontal tornado swirled around us–and we at its eye.

Alla-wuz came up beside me. "You really would have gone him, punched him, for me?"

"Yeah."

"You might as well tried to take on a mountain, you know."

There didn't seem to be a lot to say, so I kept my peace.

"Best buds forever?"

"You betcha!!" I answered to the person at my side, and all was right again with the world.

Alla-wuz, from behind, came up beside me, and froze. "I was about to ask you if you'd fight the grey when I was dying–but I think I did that before..."

"We just passed that rock twenty seconds ago..."

We shouted, "Afra, it's happening again."

"No fire, no honour. be courageous, and stick together. The times are perilous."

"Why so perilous?"

"The time jumps are not evenly spread. One area may jump back by two minutes, an adjacent area by 20 minutes. Minimizing spread-area facilitates effective optimal solution of the instant difficulty."

"Door going it a yen–the big words," said Tahla.

The grey blinked and sighed, "Always in a crisis I . . ." and he tut-tutted. "Stick close together, children. The time jumps aren't evenly spread." And our feet click-clacked on the stone path at the bottom of a long hill. Alla-wuz and I didn't want to goof–the hill was way too long. We stepped out bravely.

We found ourselves near a grove of trees. The grey said, "Our goal! The timeship is just five paces forwards."

Taking a step, the ship was only fifty paces distant, and our goal was in sight. More determination, more endurance.

Alla-wuz lay in front of me, doughnut hole in his middle. I leant beside him to tell him all would be well. Suddenly he screamed in agony, screamed at me. Intense pain clouded his face and he swore at me to leave, to flee, that I was never his friend.

Pain was talking. I blinked at the onslaught. In agony he yelled at me.

And the snake tore into Alla-wuz, and he fell, kicking me in the stomach as he fell, screaming hate at me.

And it was too much. I turned away, I raised up my eyes to a mountain of pain, and ran.

And I pushed up from my feet, turning away, and I raised up my eyes to a mountain of pain, and I lifted up my eyes to a mountain of pain and ran.

Eight giant fleeing steps of pain.

Eight footfalls punctuating the tearing confusion.

And I stopped and looked back at Alla-wuz.

Time jump, and Allla-wuz was whole, looking around for me. My world flickered a second's reversal and froze.

Alla-wuz time-jumped again to five minutes before, complete, and, looking for a friend to praise, to say "Thank you."

Time jump ripped him and the others and they were fifty paces distant and near the grove.

I was alone, fifty eternities behind.

Chapter 150
WIT'S END

The battle became a mountain brooding over we three. Gedathel, his father, and I stood, doing all our duty. Axe and mallet descended on the fell beings, sword and shield glinted, feinted, slid in, slid out the greenness and gasping, but the day was a mountain too big to see the summit, too severe to allow a slackened effort. Red miasma danced in corners of eyes, tiredness lurked at edges of muscles, humming a potent lullaby. Adrenalin fought it, pulse and fervour pushed the bounds like tired elastic, and self-subjugation clambered on towards an impossible peak.

How many had come at me that day? How many had come who had wanted my soul, had wanted to pour my life away life dishwater, had come, desiring to shred my life, my aspirations, my goals. my me-ness? Beneath, the ground was slippery, through the sheer volume of aliens dead that day.

The sun reached the mountains in the distance, muzzled its snout against them affectionately, slavishly, with abandonment of all dignity, yielded itself to their will, and slipped behind them like some whipped dog slipping behind the man to whom it had always so willingly submitted.

Never be a dog, I thought, and my whole being rebelled against the yielding to anything less than what would hold my sky, soar my future, and hold me in rightness, in righteousness, in purity of intention, love and succour.

How many more?? O Doctor, O Doctor, how many more??

"What possible point?" Fatigue stood at my elbow. "What possible point in fighting and striving, sweating amidst the dying? What possible purpose in the Lattice immersing me in some suspended agony of anticipation, struggle, possible victory and then plunged back into some new epitome of threat. What point to persevere under trial?

No, you persevere under trial because of the relationship you hold. And the one who holds the relationship succours you—the thought slowly unravelled into a truth, tautology, an essence and elixir midst the battle, a tonic for suspended hopes and dreams and goals as one struggled with buckling force, with slicing dicing knives thrown, with the cry of hope dashed (or deferred) again and again and again, until the body almost rebels, the mind seeks to divorce itself even momentarily from the situation, to rebel with vigour, to rebel with anger, to rebel because it's not right, the situation is not right, the being confronting me is not right, the life I live is not right, is not good, is not...

The body rebels.

And the earth rebelled as the sun sighed, whipped. And out from a thousand holes came a thousand night creatures, rebelling against the green things that threatened their home, their earth, their birthright—out from home, from den, from lair, from roost and eyrie they came, with little to offer except everything. Plunging at rippling green hollow bubbles with claw and tooth, they tore and ripped each fragile encasing until it ran away, fleeing into the earth to escape their dread attack. And diving as two or three within one unit, eagle and wolf and badger tore at advancing soldiers. And with enough punctures, each green rippled and fled.

The bubbled green field became a field, became a morass, became a trampled once-beautiful slight depression in a mountain that had seen ten thousand sunrises of hope and rejoicing and rewarded perseverances.

The father bowed to the creatures, now only dim in the twilight. "Our lives enwrapped in your lives—a vow sustained throughout generations, from my son, and his sons' sons, and theirs, and theirs of theirs, to you, O noble races."

"Hear, bipeds," quoth the eagle, their leader, "For our part, we have watched from our safe holes and high places your battle this day, your striving for rightness, your holding back of a fell enemy, your remaining for the sake of the living life of the planet, and we make pledge, a suzerainty, a binding agreement between us and you, that we will keep vigilance, for such is perseverance's cost, against the green ones. We will keep it with our teeth, with our claws, with our spurs and poisoned tails. We will tear at the fragile green empty linings until each dies its death. And you, as the two crafters of this planet..." An aide at his side cleared his throat, and whispered in his ear.

"Sorry," continued the eagle, "as the tool crafters of this planet, build well, construct with thought, hold rightness above profit . . . Build so the earth prospers, so both our people prosper, so that evil is held back, not promulgated. This two -pronged pledge me make between us and you."

Hear-hear's came from around us, above us, and from something that had curled up near my feet.

Gedathel's father, together with Gedathel, cried, "Between our people and yours, we hold this trust."

The animals slowly faded into the darkness, and we then breathed.

Chapter 151
'NEATH THE SWARM

There was a spiralling break in the black swirl
and into the crack

into the crack teased, eased, coalesced a techno-snake. The battle too thick elsewhere, the whirling lights had left him, for this instant of fluid space-time, unhindered. At speed he approached, stopping two feet away, spluttering and sparking.

With an acrid smell that burnt the sinuses, the sparking intensified; sparked, moulded and shaped; sparked and an electric wind pushed away from him and rushed past my face. Sparked and formed into Jort.

The not-Jort stood before me, shimmering. "Did you think I turned?" came from its direction, the lips out of synch with the sound.

Wind ceased, and we stood, old enemies in the midst of a swirl of lights. Behind me, four figures, I guessed, raced for the craft.

But the un-thing in front of me shimmered, spluttered, held my attention.

"I never turned. The thing behind you is an irreal manifestation, an extrusion into this reality of something other," and the un-thing lifted off the ground and floated two feet away, just slightly out of vertical.

"I have seen death, photographed death, tasted death. And you have become death," and sparks burning, burning, plunged from it into the ground near my feet. "But . . ." and he drifted back to the ground, a little further back, "but first, to show you how things proceed beyond the whirling battle here . . ."

Un-Jort's chest and stomach spluttered, clanked, tuned itself on, became s shiny black surface into which the vertigo of the swirling stars made me feel I could fall.

"Confused, little one? View your mother," and the black surface cleared to an image of a woman in pain. Wiping the blood from . . .

Wiping the blood

Wiping the blood from her face

Wiping the blood from the gash above the eyes, she

Wiping and wiping, she sobbed, "Son, I'm sorry. We've been so wrong. I've told you wrong. The Doctor hurts. See . . .

"And the image swirled to show the head of my father re-attaching to shoulder, body and legs–all coming together, and hands connecting to arms connecting to torso and the Doctor stood guiding them. Then the reversing, the Doctor ripping hands from arms from torso, body and legs becoming unsinewed, unconnected, and cries of pain.

Somehow the grey's voice floated back from twenty feet (I guessed) behind me. "You know your relationship with the Doctor? Wasn't he always the truest friend?"

And my mind remembered (while eyes screamed), that he had been there, Aider had been there, the son died for me.

And I steadied. Breathed. Found whiteness to ease the blackness in my eyes. Truth to cover what must only be a mist.

"Are you sure?" queried un-Jort, twisting slightly sideways. Somehow the video image stayed untouched, stayed horizontal. Jort swung back and forward like a pendulum around the stable video image.

"Are you sure? I can save your father, your mother–but you have to release yourself." A smile: "Let me in?"

And the image shifted, so Jort became my mother, as beautiful as always, pleading, crying to me, "Let him in!" Sobbing as if her heart might break.

"I, I . . ." and lips felt thick. Reality was too much to bear.

"Let him in!" and Dad stood before me. "Then we can play, can go to the park, get that norse . . ."

"I, I . . ." and the grey one called, "Remember the times with the Doctor."

To put all in the Doctor's hand, nothing to the Adder . . . dare I?

For mother, for father?

I trembled and fell to my knees.

Choices, choices too big for six years.

I groaned, "Somehow I trust . . .", and lifting rippling eyes up, rippling through tears. Three pinpoint stars, or one or two–the ripples cascaded over images from outside me–sped from behind and to the left of un-Jort, smashed into it, and propelled it over by its left shoulder.

Twirling, un-Jort broke apart into Adder, and then was pushed out at speed, propelled as a steam train, propelled as light, through the swirling stars around us, and was gone. . . .

Ripples in eyes, shaking in soul, weak at the knees. somehow I stood, searched for the others.

Somehow

somehow,

a time jump, a gasp

a running as wind

I caught up with them. amd Jort play-punched me, "Where you been? You got a broken leg? You got cut up? You been sleeping?"

I smiled shakily, and suddenly we and Alla-wuz and I were at the craft.

It powered up.

We slipped away.

Chapter 152
A FAREWELL

And Gedathel, his father, and I approached our fallen comrade, the war having fled away. Our fragility hung from hearts over the hewing of a rough funeral cairn for eyes that like pools had faded their way to a sunset, telling of the weft and the warp; of the ephermeral translaucence falling into opacity; of an absence of strength, breath having faded to waste; of the inpermanence of relationships beneath this sun.

I brooded. "Each creasing of a baby's chubby face foretells a shaving away of the fat and flesh into the shaping of a shull, so that the last of the flesh falls away in time to show bleached bones and a spirit having already flown to its Maker.

"The setting forth of a ship, flesh sails pulling before the wind, skimming the waves, turning gracefully almost on a point, shining the wavetips under the seagull, who exults in the effulgence, the water, the rightness of the vigours of life. Soon, the sails wear, the pitch coating the boards , the pitch holding back the waters wearing faster than is replaced, till at last, sails shredded wave us onwards to a better land–the seagull just a foretaste of something bigger, the exulting of the turning of the ship's body under and above the sun glistening above and on the water just a feeble echo of a more beautiful revelling, a greater soaring, a more assured shaping of life, of clutching vigour, of holding the Maker's life in our hand, knowing it to be there forever–and He there, and we in His hand and heart forever.

And the 'ecstatic bubble when you think the Maker is there' is no match for the quiet aloneness with Him each day and the knowledge that in a situation requiring courage, he is always there when fear comes like a chilling torrent to sweep you away– the knowledge of the there-ness of the Maker stays with you.

And we three built that cairn of stones, mumbled the funeral litany at first, then with greater feeling as the fiery words bit:-

> *To find oneself one's own individual,*
> *Forged by fire, and to know*
> *I stand individual, free and strong,*
> *Formed as his idea. his making,*
> *Perfect in my kind, perfect in his shapings,*
> *Being always poured out, yet never thirsty,*
> *Giving strength, yet never strengthless,*
> *Sustaining others, sustained by Him–*
> *Such in this life, such in the next.*

The truth of every man is the Maker made perfect in him.

And we turned as the sunset kissed the distant mountain, and walked from that place.
"Game Over" rippled in front of my eyes.

And in a daze, I returned to the exterior world, with the Lattice dancing at the periphery of my vision.

Chapter 153
GREY ON GREY

We stood outside the timecraft in another peaceful nook. Afra turned to us, "I go! Gladly I am no longer needed here–the team is strong again"–and his eyes rested gently on Alla-wuz and then on me.

"But shortly, one like myself will come. He will be a grey (as you call me) from the present day. His world is under the domination of something like the techno-snakes and he is searching desperately for something, anything to give hope, to see the end of their domination–or even just for something to hold to when the world rots away under his watching eye. Welcome him," and just for a moment, his eye rested on Alla-wuz. "He will be distrusting, in pain, despairing of any promise offered–but let him know you.'

"But why you just go back yourselves, your future-selves, and tell him, talk to him?"

"It is not allowed. A temporal war–for they would fight us, would force a civil war within our species of different time periods– would be catastrophic. Grandchildren would fight their grandfathers as young men... Enmity between what you are and what you would become– and to do it all within rippling alternities . . . No, it is better they not know we are here, nor that such temporal technology exists. To let them know commences disaster's diatribe."

"And now, soldiers," and he clicked his heels and saluted, gave a half-smile, "I believe that movement is the customary one on your world, it has been a pleasure to serve with you. You have acquitted yourself well, all of you," and his eye rested gently on me for a moment. "There have been soldiers on so many worlds, in so many campaigns, who have done very much less well." I thought frantically as to whether that worked out to be a compliment, and decided it was.

"As you follow the Doctor and the will he reveals for you on this planet, remember there is no violence," and his eye this time rested gently on Jort, "There is love, giving, and yet at the same time, alertness, not naivety."

"And now, having studied the effects of the past week's events and consequent problems very closely for some time, my civilization has authorised me to give a gift. I will roll back the last days so that none of the pain experienced by family, friends, believers will have occurred. The reversal will take effect as soon as I leave, children."

"The techno-snakes—will the planet ever be free of them?"

"You are already free. Anyone can be so. All they need is the Doctor—the rest is his work according to his nature and unfolding daily grace.

"And now I go. Goodbye, children, each of you. And always welcome strangers— especially one."

He boarded, and the ship rippled and vanished.

Then quickly following, a larger ripple.

A group of girls appeared and walked past on one side. Two of them looked at us, giggled. We looked down at the torn and dirty clothes, mud on our knees.

(Why are guys always oblivious of dirt until near a woman?)

Moving shamefacedly away, we decided to make for my house.

Chapter 154
MOTHER SPIT

Piling in through my front door at 7 am, we startled Mum. Still she asked pleasantly enough, "Why, hello all of you. Does any one want a drink? Have you had some breakfast?" (though the glassy look in her eye promised pain later). "It's as well that you all go back to school tomorrow. It'll take that long to get some of the mud off."

"You mean school starts tomorrow?"

"Sure! What, haven't you noticed the big holiday you're just finishing? Hmm?" Mum got that steely look that Mums get when worrying about the health of offspring.

She came close to me, found a lunge hunk of mother-saliva and rubbed hard on my face. "You've got black under your eyes—that bit's not dust, at least… Did you stay up late watching a movie or something? Nothing else was happening…"

My smile must have suddenly been too wide, "Yes, nothing was on last night—or the night before."

Alla-wuz choked a little—it could have been a laugh or a cry of pain—it was hard to tell. Fortunately, Mum's back was to him.

"Being up late is something beyond your years. Next you'll think you're big enough to change the world."

There was a thundering as Alla-wuz ran for the door. He exited somehow.

From outside came roars of laughter or cries of pain…

but I decided it was laughter. Definitely laughter.

Chapter 155
JELLY SET

It was early, oh so early, and the classroom gaped at Mrs Falpub in black misery–silence poured too easily into the aching void. If only she hadn't had that dream last night–the one where she awoke trembling at the sudden loss of something big, of something life-completing, of something too too near her to be named.

She had stumbled up, and had tried to lose herself in preparing notes for her class–the maths sheets needed improving and she had immersed herself mercilessly in them. Then, tend to Mother when she rose, give her the vital government-supplied drugs only available to approved citizens, and to school. Immerse, soak and drown, immerse, soak, and drown the ache away.

And yet, and yet, half an hour later, she was blubbering like a stunned puppy. She crossed to the window and stared across the road.

There were grey days and black days, and this could well be the blackest yet. He was somewhere in the city, she knew, and was about the Doctor's work–too much in love with Him to care to hide his commitment away, for him to toe the safe Government line. She had had no choice–lose the safety of being a good citizen, and she would lose those precious drugs which kept Mum alive.

But still she remembered the magic of two lips on a summer night, the flower scent heavy in the air…

The dream pushed back into her consciousness, bull-dozed happiness. She remembered how in the dream he had knelt, he had covered her with a blanket of perfect warmth. Then he had turned, he had turned to leave with the Doctor, and he caught a blanket thread on his shoe clasp as he turned, as he left, and she had called out but the blanket unravelled unravelled until the cold poured in.

She had awoken then. But somehow falling asleep again, dreamed and it seemed that he had filled her soul with perfect fluid sweetness, with completion; but he turned to go, he turned to go with the Doctor and he knocked the bath plug holding in all the warmth, the glory–and slowly it drained to emptiness.

And again he came and filled her lungs with dancing vitality, with dances, until turning to leave, he left the air that she needed suddenly deadened, thickening, turning to jelly.

Breathing, then not breathing … then not breathing … then gasping, she awoke in cold sweat to a room empty, a room of dead air, a room of coldness, a room of choking uselessness and trembling.

He had heard the Doctor's call, and she could not follow and he had kissed her, kissed as he left.

She had felt heaviness then, but this growing emptiness filled her days and more—a soul tasting little warmth, only feeling duty and tending others, but never, never herself.

She paused…

A familiar shape stood at the school gates, stood vacant of intention, stood too lost to try to find anything, anyone.

Him! It was him, and she
out of the room
along the corridor
and she runs down
and she runs down the stairs
and she runs down the stairs, toward
a familiar figure
a figure carrying a thousand daydreams and aching moments
and she runs
a pounding of heartbeats
…
two sets of heartbeats
and she runs
and the embracing
and the embracing
the holding
the resting of a thousand days of hoping although, although alone
and a pulling of sorrow away, as if a blanket ready for washing
and a meeting and a holding
A staying

Chapter 156
AT THE LAST

And he

will

wipe away

every
every

tear–

sometimes sooner,

and
sometimes
a little later

APPENDIX

Comments and Keys to "Tahla Expounds"

There may be some concern about using spoonerisms felt by believers jealous of God's name and honour. Spoonerisms are used occasionally in Sunday Schools, and care has been taken to ensure that even in the spoonerized text there is enough to show reverence for God without needing to decode the message to find it.

Could I suggest that the reader would read the spoonerism, laugh, half-instinctively try to puzzle out what it could be, they may even like to look up the key at the back of the book to discover what it is–thus they are paying some positive attention to a good message in the well-loved spoonerism.

It takes the Bible and puts its message in to a form that people can interact with, with enjoyment.

When constructing spoonerisms, the author swapped consonants between same or different words. It was fair game to put the same consonant in more than one place–and just simply dispose of the other consonant. And once the new word had been made and it sounded like a known English word, I considered it OK to simply write the known English word for the sake of humour, eg see-staw would probably be heard as seesaw, so I wrote it as seesaw.

Chapter 27
I was wondering . . . would you like to go to the park to play?
They're always there for us, like when the son fixed me after the bubble.
He's a beauty, isn't he?
If the Doctor is able to raise his son from the dead, doesn't he fully rule? We can really trust the Doctor to provide for us.
He doesn't do it just for us. His giving is so we can give to others.

Chapter 31
Too much perfume, I think..
My name is Tahla.

Chapter 34

Let not your hearts be trembled.
Believe in the Doctor, believe in the Son.
In the Doctor's place are twenty hundred rooms.
If it were not so, I would have told you.
He goes to prepare a place for us,
And if he goes to prepare a place for us,
He will take us home to the son!
That where he is, there we may stay as well.
Blessed dimension, blessed place.

Chapter 36

These are good, Amah
Yes, tubey full
These sandwiches are good
These have dill and chutney too.
Dill
Once I liked cheese and ham. Then it was peanut butter. Oh, after that it was strawberry jam. But later at my house, we has these type
No, later mum had us all have this
No, Later mum decided to have dill.

Chapter 40

The Doctor's a loving shepherd.
I have everything I need.
He makes me lie down in green pastures.
He restores my soul. He guides in right paths for His Name's sake.
Although I walk in the valley of shadow of death,
I will not fear, for the Doctor is with me.
Your shepherd's rod and your staff power and protect me.
You prepare a pan-bake for me
And welcome me as an honoured gent.
Surely goodness and mercy shall
follow me down the lanes in my life.
I'll die in the health of my soul.
Health forever! Amen.

Chapter 43

Lo, I tell you mysteries. We will not all sleep, but we shall all be changed in a moment, in the twinkling of an eye, at the last trumpet. For the trumpet shall sound, sound, and the dead shall be raised in victory.

Behold, the death is swallowed up in victory!!

The death is swallowed up in victory.

Chapter 47

Without danger putting it out, the mystery of the Doctor is tremendous–

He who was shown in a flourish,

Proven by the aider;

Seen by the unseen world;

Discussed oft with neighbours;

Accepted with love by the world;

Now risen to his glory.

Chapter 48

The Doctor is our resting and stronghold,

A mainstay anytime.

I will not fear foes, though the world should change,

Though the mountains should shake in the heart of the sea,

its waters growl, roar and foam.

Even if a fellow worker understands change better than me

And is promoted while I demote,

if a chosen career is irrelevant after a change...

Even if at the end of life, there is nothing to show but that

I did fruitfully in an outdated job.

I shall smile;

For the Doctor is a loving shepherd

Chapter 52

For he is the loving Doctor

enduring forever.

His Kingdom shall never be destroyed;

His rule will never be put away.

Deliveries and saves are made by he

who saved Daniel from harm, from
the power of the big lions.

Chapter 54
Scared my mum, though.

Chapter 56
I know that you can do all things, and that no purpose
of yours can be stopped. You do according to your
will, in the army of the heaven and the inhabitants of the
earth. No one can restrain your hand. You, who sit in the
heavens laugh, have rebel kings and rulers in derision.
Whenever kings strive, vehemently decide to change,
you change, yourself—can suddenly come about, rulers
are deposed of, new ones are set up.

And yet, the very
same one came humbly, bringing
good news in your street and in your towns.

Yes, the Doctor cleans up the earth.

Chapter 57
Yeah, ran into any good balls lately?

Chapter 60
Beloved, do not be afraid of the
Fiery trial which is to come.
Stand in the faith!

Chapter 62
Quit you like men! Be strong! Rejoice
always, give thanks in all things.
Be always in prayer for all the saints

Chapter 63
We walk by faith,
Not by sight.

Chapter 75
Behold I come swiftly…
"Hold fast that which you have
So that none can take your crown
(reward)."
To him who overcomes, I will
Make like a column in the House of the Doctor.

Chapter 79
And I'm just so glad to be back.
I wanted to see you looney guys.
Was Mrs Falpub cranky yesterday?
We had such a good time! I went to the sea side.
The seaside was great! It was just Dad and me. We slept in a tent and we got up early every morning! Straight away we plunged into the breakers. Kestrels flew above us! I loved the crabs and sandbar–fish, too! I caught a bream and, and box jelly–and he rolled his eyes in disgust–We threw that back. But every day was just as good as that.
My back was sore.
Dad was chasing me. I stumbled, jumped three steps, caught my foot in a hole–and bam!! Then I got a sore back.

Chapter 123
You with him now?
So you don't fight the Doctor's followers?
But why–why now?
How could you know that? Actually its "Blessed are those who create peace; the same men shall be blessed."–the other is just silly . . . But how, how could you know? I never have written any thing to paper.
Pardon?
Let's go!

Chapter 131
And I found a book I borrowed from our town library last year which had had the last part ripped out, and I was able to...

Chapter 147
Why are they doing this?
And what are these?

Chapter 149
You're doing it again–the big words

For more information or requests email the publisher at: info@advbooks.com
or
visit Greg and Kathy Weller's website: www.gregkathyweller.com

To purchase additional copies of this book, visit our bookstore website at:
www.advbookstore.com

"we bring dreams to life"™
www.advbookstore.com